Norman Maclean

Memoir of Marshal Keith

With a sketch of the Keith family

Norman Maclean

Memoir of Marshal Keith
With a sketch of the Keith family

ISBN/EAN: 9783337382032

Printed in Europe, USA, Canada, Australia, Japan

Cover: Foto ©Andreas Hilbeck / pixelio.de

More available books at **www.hansebooks.com**

MEMOIR

OF

MARSHAL KEITH,

WITH A

SKETCH OF THE KEITH FAMILY.

By a Peterheadian.

PETERHEAD: DAVID SCOTT.
ABERDEEN: ROBERT WALKER.

1869.

TO

His Most Gracious Majesty William,

KING OF PRUSSIA,

THE MUNIFICENT DONOR OF THE STATUE OF MARSHAL
KEITH TO THE TOWN OF PETERHEAD,

THIS MEMOIR

OF ONE OF THE BRAVEST GENERALS OF HIS
NOBLE ANCESTOR,

FREDERICK THE GREAT,

IS BY PERMISSION

RESPECTFULLY DEDICATED.

BY

THE AUTHOR.

PREFACE.

No apology is necessary for writing the lives of two of the most remarkable men that were ever banished from their native country. The fragrance of their memory is still fresh in the land of their adoption, and it would be a national disgrace if it were not so in this, the land which gave them birth.

Though the Author has been indebted to various works for part of the materials contained in the following pages, the reader will, it is hoped, find new facts which help to clear up certain periods in the lives of the last of the Keiths, which, to say the least, have been down to the present time somewhat hazy. Restricted to certain limits, the Author has, nevertheless, been careful to select such information as he deems most interesting, and which bears more directly on the history of the brothers George and James. At another time, he may prepare a more elaborate life of the men whom " the great soldier of the age" honoured with the name of friend.

It is but right to state that, though the authenticity of the MS. mentioned in the introduction has been vouched for by the late Peter Buchan, the statements contained in the early part are open to be questioned. The popular belief that the Keith coat-of-arms was acquired so early as 1006 must be set aside, when we find Cosmo Innes, in his *Sketches of Early Scotch History*, writing thus :—"The introduction of heraldry was, in all countries, quickly followed by the adoption of the shields of arms as the appropriate distinction of seals. This cannot be said to have commenced in Scotland earlier than the reign of William the Lion (1165—1214). Even during that reign, the practice was by no means general. William himself, and some persons of great distinction, both Saxon and Norman, though evidently following the knightly customs of the age, had not yet adopted fixed family arms." In almost every old family, we find its representatives ready to trace the origin of their arms to some great achievement on the part of some ancestor. Wherever it has been possible to investigate these, the legends in connection with them have been found to be, in a great measure, fabrications. It was only at a much later period, and in very rare instances, that such commemorative marks were allowed to be added. However, as it is interesting, being the earliest account we have of the family, it has been given, leaving the reader to form his own conclusions.

To honour the memory of the dead, to sketch truthfully the career of the two men whose crumbling castles stand in our midst,—and around which cling our sunniest memories,—and to raise to them "a monument more durable than brass," has been the small but honest endeavour of

THE AUTHOR.

CONTENTS.

MEMOIR

OF

MARSHAL KEITH,

WITH

A Sketch of the Keith Family.

· INTRODUCTION.

SCARCELY any district in the whole empire can lay claim to greater honour than Buchan. For centuries it was the residence of two of the highest dignitaries in the state— the Marischal and the Constable of the kingdom,—the one vested in the Keiths of Inverugie, the other in the Hays of Slains. It also gave birth, at no very distant period, to two of the greatest warriors of modern times; men who helped, in a very considerable degree, to form two of the most powerful empires of Europe—Russia and Prussia. The former of these was General Gordon, born in the bleak, treeless, and clayey district of Cruden, and brought up at its parish school. Like the place from which he came, he was, in character, stern and severe; and, on this

B

account, better able to cope with the half-savage people of
Russia, and their still more savage master, Peter the Great.
Being a younger son, and a Roman Catholic, he had early
to seek his fortune ; and, after great hardships and strange
vicissitudes, found at last the work suited for him in the
new and rising empire of all the Russias.   After securing
to its future great ruler the supreme power at a most
critical period, and governing the country in his absence,
this illustrious Scotchman died, leaving his impress on
Russia and Europe.   Feeling the mighty loss he was
about to sustain, "the Czar, who had visited him four
times in his illness, and had been twice with him during
the night, stood weeping by his bed as he drew his last
breath ; and the eyes of him who had left Scotland a poor,
unbefriended wanderer, were closed by the hands of an
Emperor."   The latter was James Francis Edward Keith,
Field-Marshal in the Prussian service.   At bonnie Inverugie, one of the hereditary seats of the family, the future
Marshal was born ; and from this place, with a sad heart
and light purse, went forth the last of the Marischals.
The elder, the representative of a noble race that had for
seven centuries held the foremost place in Scotland, left
his native land an exile, on account of his adherence to
the royal house of Stuart, in the unfortunate rising of
1715,   For the rest of his life, he wandered about the Continent, living at various courts, the intimate friend of princes
and the beloved of kings.   His brother, a born soldier,
and of such military renown that his services were sought
after by the greatest powers of Europe, after fighting his

way to the highest distinction that could be accorded him, and helping to form the then growing country of Prussia, died on the field of Hochkirchen, respected by his enemies, and bewailed by his master and close companion, Frederick the Great.

It is with the last two that we intend, at present, to deal, and to sketch briefly their distinguished and glorious career in a foreign land.

THE KEITH FAMILY.

The origin of the ancient family of Keith is, as is usual in such cases, shrouded in mystery, or entirely dependent upon the traditions which have been handed down from generation to generation. According to an ancient MS., preserved in the family until the rebellion of 1715 (the authenticity of which is most positively vouched for by a no mean authority in such matters, Peter Buchan, author of the "Ballads of the North-East Coast of Scotland"), the family came originally from Germany. They were a branch of the Catti, who, having been driven from their homes, and from various parts of the Continent, at last took to their ships, and were driven on that part of Scotland called after them Cattyness or Caithness. Here, being as badly treated as on the mainland, they were forced, after desperate engagements with the natives, to the hills and woods, where they managed, for a time, to live free from all molestation. They gradually spread over the country, forming families, increasing in number and importance, and invariably obeying one chief, who was looked upon as the head of the Clan Chatti. This, in modern times, was changed into the Clan Chattan ; while, after various modifications, the family name came to be retained as Keth or Keith.

Whether this account can be depended upon or not, this at least is certain, that the family became famous in history during the reign of Malcolm the Second. At a battle with the Danes, near a place called Camus or Camestown, in Angus, the victory was gained by the Scots, mainly through the prowess of Robert, the head of the Keiths, who slew, with his own hand, Camus, the leader of the Danes. For this gallant action, the king conferred upon him, and his posterity, the land in East Lothian which ever after bore their name. He also appointed him hereditary Grand Marischal of Scotland, which high office continued in the family till 1715. It was in this battle that the family acquired their motto and shield. According to one account, the king, after viewing the dead body of Camus, dipped his three fingers in the blood of his fallen foe, and drew three strokes or pales on Robert's shield ; and, as the latter had declared previous to the battle that God would grant them the victory, because the savages had demolished his houses and despised his services, he gave him as his motto *Veritas Vincit*, Truth Conquers. According to another, one of the noblemen, disputing the death of Camus, was challenged to single combat by the chief of the Catti, and being slain by him, the king, dipping three of his fingers in the blood of the nobleman, gave expression to the motto which the family ever afterwards bore. This chief, knighted by the king, married Margaret Fraser, daughter of Simon Fraser of Tweedale, and from him, undoubtedly, was descended the race of the Keiths so well known in Scottish history.

Farther on, we find Sir Robert Keith high in the confidence of King Edward I. of England, and keeping his allegiance to him after Bruce was crowned king of Scotland. He, however, joined that prince previous to the battle of Bannockburn, where he commanded the cavalry ; and, by a well-timed charge, led the way to that famous victory. With a wisdom, prudence, and policy characteristic of him, King Robert granted to this noble family part of the lands in Aberdeenshire called Buchan, formerly possessed by his enemy, the Comyn. Thus was a family, with its friends, retainers, and vassals well disposed to the king, planted in a part of the country which had been long hostile to him ; and, by their intermarriages with the inhabitants, finally removed any bad feeling which may have existed towards him, and, in time, " formed a people attached to the crown, the liberties, and laws of the kingdom."

Through a marriage with one of the co-heiresses of Sir Alexander Fraser, Chamberlain of Scotland, Bruce's brother-in-law, the Keiths further acquired great estates in Kincardineshire ; and, having added to them the rock of Dunottar, built upon it an extensive castle, which was afterwards their chief seat.

In 1458, the family was ennobled in the person of Sir William Keith, who was created Earl Marischal and Lord Keith. His house reached its highest pitch of power in the person of his great-great-grandson, the fourth Earl, called William of the Tower, because he lived in such seclusion at Dunottar. "By marriage with his kinswoman, the co-heiress of Inverugie, he nearly doubled the family domains, which now included lands in seven shires— Haddington, Linlithgow, Kincardine, Aberdeen, Banff, Elgin, and Caithness. He was reputed the wealthiest peer in Scotland, having a rental of 270,000 merks a year, and being able, it was boasted, to travel from the Tweed to the Pentland Firth, eating every meal and sleeping every night on his own lands." He was a zealous promoter of the Reformation ; and, by a well-timed speech, caused the Confession of Faith, when presented to the Parliament, to be " approved of and authorised, and the Reformation settled." It is said that, by his " magnificent living, and the vast charges he had been at in public office, he had drawn his estate into considerable burden. When he began to reflect upon this, he was galled that an ancient family and great fortune should suffer any decay in his person, and therefore confined himself to his castle of Dunottar till his debts were thereby paid, where he continued the space of seventeen years and some months, and so improved his fortune that it exceeded any possessed by a Scot's subject."

These vast possessions passed to his grandson, George, the fifth Earl, who, after spending some time on the

Continent, acquainting himself with the politics, civilities, and languages óf the various countries, returned to his native land to be engaged in affairs of the greatest moment. So high an opinion had James VI. of his merit, that he fixed upon him as the fittest person to go, as ambassador, to Denmark to accomplish his marriage with Anne, and to bring her to Scotland. In this embassy, "he behaved to the great admiration of the Danes, and the glory of the Scottish nation;" and, on his return, received the thanks of the king and the nation. This affair, however, greatly diminished his great fortune, and to this day his expenses remain a debt on the country. He took a great interest in the reformation and cultivation of the country; and, to advance the progress of learning in the north, founded Marischal College, Aberdeen, in the year 1593. He endowed it with the privileges of a University; and, out of his own income, bestowed a sum sufficient for the maintenance of a Principal and three Professors. In the same year, he granted a charter to the town of Peterhead, evidently considering that it would be the means of developing the resources of the district, an excellent place for export and import trade with the Continent, and, from its natural position, likely, in time, to become a town of importance. In a great measure, these hopes have been realised. Having been appointed by the king Lieutenant of the north, during the disturbances caused by the Spanish plot, in the year 1593, when some of the nobility even were in arms, he acted so judiciously, and with such firmness, that he entirely suppressed the threatened

insurrection without shedding one drop of blood, and gained
for himself much praise, both from the king and the people.
In all the great actions of the time, his name appears; and,
as the highest mark of honour which he could confer upon
him, James clothed him with royal authority, and made
him Commissioner to the Scottish Parliament, in the year
1607.   He died at Dunottar, and was buried at St. Bride's,
where his Latin epitaph, detailing his glorious life, may
still be seen.

In the reign of Queen Anne, we find another of the
Earls—a man so generous and liberal, and so magnificent
in his way of living, that he considerably impaired his
fortune—upholding the dignity of his ancient family,
zealously opposing the Union of the two kingdoms, and
entering the following spirited protest against it :—

"I do hereby protest that whatever is contained in any article of
the treaty of Union betwixt Scotland and England shall in no manner
of way derogate from, or be prejudicial to, me or my successors in
our heritable office of Great Marischal of Scotland in all time coming,
or in full and free enjoyment and exercise of the whole rights,
dignities, titles, honours, powers, and privileges thereto belonging,
which my ancestors and I have possessed and exercised as rights of
property these 700 years: And I do further protest that the
Parliament of Scotland, and Constitution thereof, may remain and
continue as formerly: And I desire this, my protestation, may be
inserted in the minutes, and recorded in the books of Parliament,
and thereupon taken instruments."

This was the father of the two last of the race, the
subjects of our present sketch—George, Earl Marischal ;
and his still more distinguished brother, James, Field-

Marshal in the Prussian service during the reign of the celebrated Frederick the Great.

THE TWO BROTHERS.

According to the best authorities, Earl Marischal was born on the 2d of April, old style, 1693. It is conjectured that the event took place at Inverugie, though no conclusive proof can be brought forward for this belief. The precise date of the birth of his brother is also a matter of dispute ; but, that the event took place at Inverugie, admits not of a doubt. According to the baptismal register of St. Fergus, in which parish the castle is situated, he was baptised on the 16th of June, 1696. Here the Earl and the future Marshal—varied by occasional visits to Dunottar, that castle by the sea—amused themselves playing around the banks of the lovely Ugie, or fishing in that excellent trouting stream. To this day, a stone, near the mouth of this small river, is pointed out from which the Earl and his companions used to cast their lines when the tide was full. Happy days these were, often recalled by them when exiles in a distant land, and far from bonnie Inverugie.

It must be allowed, however, that such peaceful and innocent occupations were often diversified, chiefly on the part of the younger brother, by affairs of more stirring moment ; some mischievous raid, or the teasing of an old retainer of the family remarkable for his crossness and the outspokenness of his remarks. On one of these occasions, when the future Marshal had been particularly mad in his pranks, and overstepped all the old man's bounds of propriety, he cried out, shaking his head, "Oh, laddie, laddie! gin ever ye mak' a puddin', I'll eat the prick!" meaning a small piece of wood inserted at the end of Scotch white puddings for the purpose of keeping in the meat. In after years, when the wild boy had become a man, and risen to high rank in the country of his adoption, he is said to have sent the old man a "prick," and something more substantial, to remind him of the old days when he used to tease him by his pranks.

Traditions, handed down from generation to generation, speak of the love of the two brothers as something remarkable, and of the power of the elder and more staid over the more impulsive and mischievously-disposed Field-Marshal, as an uncommon thing. The latter was well known in the village as the ringleader in every wild freak and boyish trick; and when he got into disgrace, as was often the case, the former, by the gentleness of his disposition, the kindness of his heart, the appealingness of his words and looks, the extreme love shown for his brother in spite of his repeated delinquencies, and his ready guarantee for his future good behaviour, invariably managed to beg him off.

This love they never lost; for, when in exile, and often reduced to great straits, they kept as long as possible in each other's company; and, when at last compelled to separate, a correspondence was sustained as close as the circumstances of the time and their varied engagements would allow,—for the younger was soon deeply immersed in the troubles of a very troublous period. And, at last, when a permanent home seemed to be obtained for the one, he hastened to acquaint the other with the fact, and it required very little to prevail upon either to form the resolution of spending the remainder of their days together.

Under the able tutorship of William Meston, and their relation the celebrated Bishop Keith, the boys continued till they went to Marischal College, founded, as we have already said, by their great-grandfather. The younger was intended for the law, but his own inclination was for arms, which the influence of his mother, and the rebellion of 1715, helped to foster. When only eighteen years of age, he was called upon to decide as to his future life, and to take an active part in a contest the most unfortunate that our history presents,—a contest which never deserved the support of so many noble families, and which was too dearly purchased by the death and banishment of those whose ancestors had borne the brunt of the battle around the forms of the departed Stuarts, of whom the then representative was an unfortunate specimen.

Induced by their mother (for their father had died when the Earl was nineteen years of age), who was a fierce Jacobite, they entered upon a cause from which their more mature judgment would have dissuaded them. The Earl, on the accession of George I., before giving up the appointment of Captain of the Guard, which he had held under Queen Anne, is said to have offered to proclaim the Pretender King of England at the head of his troop,

but the timidity of the Jacobite party would not permit it.
It is right to state that this rests on very insufficient
evidence, and is altogether at variance with the Earl's
known character for prudence.   He retired, however, to
his estates in Scotland, and waited patiently for the time of
action.   It came ; but, though headed by some of the
noblest families in the land, it was, on the whole, one of
the most pitiful and disgracefully organised affairs that
could well be imagined.

THE RISING OF 1715.

On the 6th of September, 1715, the standard of
rebellion was raised at Kirkmichael, a village in Braemar,
with only sixty men ; and, while the pole was being
planted in the ground, the gilt ball fell from the top—
an augury of the future fate of many of those who
stood around, and who afterwards took part in this
rebellion.   Then, in quick succession, came the assembling
of the clans at Perth ; the meeting at Sheriffmuir ; the
drawn battle, by a wing being defeated on each side,
but with all real advantage on that of Argyle ; the
surrender of the troops at Preston ; and the subsequent
retreat to the mountain fastnesses.   And then, when all
was over, came the scenes on Towerhill, the extinction of
many a noble name, and the exile of those who would
otherwise have been an ornament to their country.

.   At the battle of Sheriffmuir, Earl Marischal, along

with his brother, commanded two squadrons on the right of the second line. Being sent forward to take possession of a rising ground on which the enemy was posted, he unexpectedly came upon them when in disorder, and, charging with great vigour, in less than ten minutes entirely defeated six regiments of foot and five squadrons of dragoons, which composed more than the half of the Duke's army. Notwithstanding this, they were greatly blamed for allowing their opponents to retire with the principal standard as a trophy.

About a month after this, on the 25th of December, Christmas-day, the man for whom they had risked their lives landed at Peterhead, without money, troops, or warlike stores. In disguise, he slept in a house, now demolished, which stood at the south end of the Longate, and next day advanced towards the headquarters of the army, lodging at Newburgh, a seat of Earl Marischal's. After passing through Aberdeen, still in disguise, he arrived at Fetteresso, where the Earl proclaimed him king in front of his castle door. There, many of them were introduced to their pseudo-sovereign for the first time, and it cannot be said that their enthusiasm was of a very glowing kind. Even though we grant that he was suffering from ague, and scarcely fit to act his part on such an occasion, it must be allowed that his appearance was anything but prepossessing, and his manner by no means engaging. He was really a poor, weak, feeble man, afraid of his own safety, selfish to the last degree, and filled with the glories of a throne which was never to be his.   . ·

But the crowning act of his folly and weakness was the desertion of his troops, without even daring to show his face before the enemy. Even supposing that their numbers were few, and their chances of success small, it was his duty to have stood by them to the last, and to have marched north with them. It is evident that James grasped eagerly at the excuses Mar brought forward for his departure, and had fully made up his mind to leave before he asked the advice of the rest. This, given by the Earl Marischal, was so sensible and telling, that, had not James been greatly deficient in moral courage and excessively selfish, he would have been shamed into embracing it. He distinctly leads them to understand that he and the rest were quite aware of the fact that the king was afraid of his own person ; but that, under the circumstances, he did not apprehend it could be in more danger than those of the rest, as he could make his escape more easily from any of the harbours in the West of Scotland than from that of Montrose, the entrance to which was guarded by two men-of-war. He also declared that it was not for the king's honour, nor for that of the nation, to thus withdraw from the contest without striking a blow. Brave and noble words these from a youth of twenty-two to his king. But they had not the desired effect ; for, that same night, the craven monarch, and the no less craven generalissimo, embarked, leaving the army to its fate, and giving orders that Lieutenant-General Gordon should assume the command in his absence. When the base desertion of their leaders became known, the effect upon the army was most disastrous. Consternation was general, and the whole body so dispirited " that," says Keith the younger, " had the Duke of Argyle followed us close and come up with only 2000 men, I'm persuaded he might have taken us all prisoners ; but he, hearing at Montrose that the king was gone, halted there a whole day, and so gave us time to get to Aberdeen."

From Aberdeen, they marched to Ruthven in Badenoch, and there disbanded the army. Some made for the mountain fastnesses, while others endeavoured to find some way out of the country. Among the latter was young Keith, who, after much fatigue (for he was wounded) and many narrow escapes, managed, along with about 100 other officers, to make his escape from the Isle of Skye in a vessel that had been sent by their craven king.

The Earl made his way to Inverugie to visit his mother, and remove such things from the Castle as would be certain to fall a prey to the royal soldiery. The family plate and other valuables were conveyed to a small hut that stood in one of the fields or parks now on the estate of Mountpleasant, and were afterwards removed, bit by bit, as they found it convenient. The dependants were dismissed, and advised to seek some place of safety, as the Castle was certain soon to be attacked and destroyed. The Earl himself, in the grey dawn of a spring morning, rode forth from the home of his fathers, never to return. How different was it from the last time, only a few months before, when his followers, drinking the health of King James in the Castle yard, threw their glasses over their

left shoulders, and marched forth confident of victory.
After proceeding a short distance, and before coming to a
bend in the road where he lost the view of the Castle, he
turned round and gazed, for the last time, on the noble
pile where his ancestors had for so long lived and held
sway. Heaving a deep sigh and dropping a tear, he
quickened his horse into a sharp trot, and, disappearing
round the angle of the road, was lost to view; and the
greater part of those who gazed upon the retreating form
of the last of the Marischals never saw him more.

After wandering about for some time, at great risk of
his life (for the Government had set a price on his head),
he managed to make his escape to the Continent. He
found his way to James, who had been granted, by the
Pope, a residence at Avignon, and soon afterwards at
Urbin. Here he remained, waiting anything favourable to
their cause. A gleam of hope shot athwart their gloomy
horizon when Charles XII., the Lion of the North,
animated with the desire of avenging himself on George I.,
who had bought from the King of Denmark the two
Duchies of Bremen and Kerdun, which he claimed as his
own, took them under his protection. The discovery of
the plot, the arrest of his emissaries, and the sudden death
of Charles at the seige of Frederichshall, put a stop to the
whole project when on the eve of execution. But more
substantial aid was promised them when Alberoni became
minister of Spain. Having declared war on England,
because she was one of the powers that had formed the
Quadruple Alliance, he invited the Keiths to the court,

and offered the rank of Lieutenant-General to the Earl,
which he refused on the plea that he did not consider
himself qualified for the post, both from age and inex-
perience. Having accepted a subordinate situation, he,
along with his brother, who had obtained a commission in
the "Irish Brigade," awaited anxiously the promised aid
which was to enable them to make good a landing in
Scotland.

THE BATTLE OF GLENSHIEL.

This aid came at last; and the expedition set out on its
mission, but completely failed, owing to the petty views
and morbid jealousies of the Jacobite leaders in Scotland.
The Earl set sail with the expedition, and landed in the
island of Lewis, where he waited the arrival of his brother,
who had been sent into France—then at war with Spain—
for the purpose of informing the Jacobites there of the
enterprise in favour of their lawful king. Having performed this secret and delicate mission with a coolness and
fertility of resource which do him great credit, he set sail ;
and, after narrowly escaping the English fleet, found the
expedition at Stornoway. Making for the mainland, they
intended to march on Inverness ; but, while they wasted
their time squabbling among themselves, and uncertain
what to do, Wightman, with a superior force, suddenly
attacked them in the Pass of Glenshiel, forced their right
and centre, and drove them to the mountains. The battle

was not decisive ; but, news having arrived of the failure
of Ormond's expedition against England, it was judged
best that the Spaniards should surrender and the High-
landers disperse. After this was done, Keith the younger,
being sick of a fever, managed, after some trouble, to ˙
embark at Peterhead, and landed at Holland, where he met
his brother, who had crossed some time before from the
Western Isles. From this place, they made their way,
with great difficulty, to Spain,—for Holland and France
were at war with that country,—being compelled to
destroy their commissions at Sedan, lest the possession of
them should bring them into trouble. Arrived there, they
immediately applied to the Minister of War to have these
renewed. Under some pretext or other, this was delayed,
until the brothers were reduced to the lowest ebb, and
were glad to accept the hospitality of some friends who
had known them in Paris.

EARL MARISCHAL'S CAREER.

After a time, the Earl made his way to Avignon, and
latterly to Rome, where the Pretender was staying, and
was engaged by him in a number of secret negotiations
between his court and those of the rest of Europe. Of
these, however, we can now find no account, as the Earl
was a particularly reserved man, who entrusted none of
his friends with any of his secrets, and destroyed all his
papers about thirty years before his death. For the

services then rendered, the Chevalier gave him the Order of the Garter, which he seldom or never wore, saying, justly, " It is necessary to renounce, under pain of ridicule, these vain ornaments, when the person from whom they are derived is not in a position to make them respected."

In 1733, when Spain declared war against the Emperor, the Earl wrote requesting to be employed in the service. This the King refused at first, on the plea that Earl Marischal was a Protestant, though, only a year before, he had raised him to a command against the Moors in Africa. While matters were pending, he took up his residence at Valencia, as he was much attached to Spain on account of the many kind friends he had there, "not to mention the sun," he jocosely remarks.   While here, he heard that his brother had been wounded at the siege of Ockzakow; and, full of as deep love and care for him as in the days of their youth, he hurried to his side to render any assistance that he could.   And it was fortunate for the wounded man that he did so; for, on his arrival, the surgeons were deliberating concerning the amputation of one of his limbs, which the Earl would not permit.   The end justified his tender regard for him; for, though, spite of his unremitting care, it took two full years before the General was restored to his usual state of health, he had, nevertheless, the pleasure of seeing his body intact. Together, they returned to France, and took up their residence at the town of Bareges, a small watering-place in the Pyrenees, where the younger brother received great advantage from the mineral water.

When his brother was sent on some diplomatic business to England, the Earl retired again to Spain, where he seems to have continued for some time.   In the year 1740, on the rupture between Great Britain and that country, he was sent, by the Chevalier, to the Spanish court to induce them to adopt measures for his restoration.   These seem, however, to have failed.   Three years afterwards, we find him at Boulogne, and one of the parties selected for the command of an expedition to be sent to Scotland, by France, in support of the Pretender.   Finding, however, that either the French Ministry or the Chevalier's agents at Paris were determined to exclude both him and the Duke of Ormond from any share in the expedition, he appears to have retired from it, after communicating with the Chevalier on the subject.   He seems to have considered, on very good grounds, that France was not to be trusted in the matter, and strongly dissuaded the young Pretender from listening to any proposals from her.   For speaking thus plainly, and also for advising him against joining the French army in Flanders, where he would have fought against Englishmen and the allies of England, the Pretender was furious, and wrote to his father at Rome to accuse and abuse the noble exile, by far the best man that ever engaged in that desperate cause.

So eager was the Prince to enter upon the great work of his life that he is said to have proposed to the Earl to embark in a herring boat, and make his way to Scotland, with characteristic trust in the ancient heroic kingdom. But, though it came to something very like this in the end, the cautious Earl, whom misfortunes had made wise, did not accept the offer. In the rising which followed—the rebellion of 1745—the Earl took no part. This seems to have been a great surprise to his friends in Scotland, and was also a source of deep regret to the Prince. We find the Prince writing thus strongly to his father on the subject, after he had landed in the country—" I find it a great loss that the brave Lord Marischal is not with me. His character is very high in this country, and must be so wherever it is known. I had rather see him as a thousand French, who, if they should come only as friends to assist your Majesty in the recovery of your just rights, the weak people would believe came as invaders." It should be remembered that this was written by one who had formerly denounced the Earl, and whose conduct had, no doubt, caused his absence from the expedition.

The Earl, again in Spain, conceiving himself to be slighted by the Minister, determined to quit the country altogether; and, after some consideration, retired to Venice, where he amused himself with his books and the company of men of literary tastes. This he left for Berlin, to live with his brother, who had entered the service of Frederick the Great. The latter, anxious to have the Earl engaged under him, sent him as ambassador to the court of France, where he continued for some years, liking the nation better than his employment. He himself says—" Alas! it is necessary for that business to have a skill which I do not possess, and which I by no means care for." At his own request, he was removed to

the Governorship of Neuchâtel, where he made the
acquaintance of Rousseau, who, spite of his cantankerous
disposition and mania for quarrelling, had not the heart,
or could not find an excuse for fighting with Earl
Marischal. In his " Confessions" we find an excellent
account of him at this time, and of the estimation in which
he was held by the people over whom he ruled. As it is
extremely interesting, we give it entire :—" On my arrival
at Motiers I had written to Lord Keith, marshal of Scotland, and governor of Neuchâtel, informing him of my
retreat into the states of his Prussian majesty, and requesting
of him his protection. He answered me with his well
known generosity, and in the manner I had expected from
him. He invited me to his house. I went with M.
Martinet, lord of the manor of Val de Travers, who was ·
in great favour with his excellency. The venerable appearance of this illustrious and virtuous Scotchman, power-
fully affected my heart, and from that instant began between
him and me the strong attachment, which on my part still
remains the same, and would be so on his, had not the
traitors, who have deprived me of all the consolations of
life, taken advantage of my absence to deceive his old age
and depreciate me in his esteem. George Keith, hereditary
marshal of Scotland, and brother to the famous General
Keith who lived gloriously and died in the bed of honour,
had quitted his country at a very early age, and was pro-
scribed on account of his attachment to the house of Stuart.
With that house, however, he soon became disgusted by
the unjust and tyrannical spirit he remarked in the ruling

character of the Stuart family. He lived a long time in
Spain, the climate of which pleased him exceedingly, and
at length attached himself, as his brother had done, to the
service of the king of Prussia, who knew men and gave
them the reception they merited. His majesty received a
great return for this reception, in the services rendered him
by Marshal Keith, and by what was infinitely more precious,
the sincere friendship of his lordship. The great mind of
this worthy man, haughty and republican, could stoop to
no other yoke than that of friendship, but to this it was so
obedient, that with very different maxims he saw nothing
but Frederic the moment he became attached to him. The
king charged the marshal with affairs of importance, sent
him to Paris, to Spain, and at length, seeing he was already
advanced in years, let him retire with the government of
Neuchâtel, and the delightful employment of passing there
the remainder of his life in rendering the inhabitants happy.
The people of Neuchâtel, whose manners are trivial, know
not how to distinguish solid merit, and suppose wit to
consist in long discourses. When they saw a sedate man
of simple manners appear amongst them, they mistook his
simplicity for haughtiness, his candour for rusticity, his
laconism for stupidity, and rejected his benevolent cares,
because, wishing to be useful, and not being a sycophant,
he knew not how to flatter people he did not esteem. In
the ridiculous affair of the minister Petitpierre, who was
displaced by his colleagues, for having been unwilling they
should be eternally damned, my Lord, opposing the usur-
pations of the ministers, saw the whole country of which

he took the part, rise up against him, and when I arrived there, the stupid murmur had not entirely subsided. He passed for a man influenced by the prejudices with which he was inspired by others, and of all the imputations brought against him it was the most devoid of truth. My first sentiment, on seeing this venerable old man, was that of tender commiseration, on account of his extreme leanness of body, years having already left him little else but skin and bone ; but, when I raised my eyes to his animated, open, noble countenance, I felt a respect, mingled with confidence which absorbed every other sentiment. He answered the very short compliment I made him when first I came into his presence by speaking of something else, as if I had already been a week in his house. He did not bid us sit down. The stupid Chatelain, the lord of the manor, remained standing. For my part I at first sight saw in the fine and piercing eye of his lordship something so conciliating that, feeling myself entirely at ease, I without ceremony took my seat by his side upon the sopha. By the familiarity of his manner I immediately perceived the liberty I took gave him pleasure, and that he said to himself : this is not a Neuchâtelois. Singular efect of the similarity of characters ! at an age when the heart loses its natural warmth, that of this old man grew warm by his attachment to me to a degree which surprised every body. He came to see me at Motiers under the pretence of quail shooting, and staid there two days without touching a gun. We conceived such a friendship for each other that we knew not how to live separate : the castle of

Colombier, where he passed the summer, was six leagues from Motiers; I went there at least once a fortnight, and made a stay of twenty-four hours, and then returned like a pilgrim with my heart full of affection for my host. The emotion I had formerly experienced in my journeys from the Hermitage to Eaubonne, was certainly very different, but it was not more pleasing than that with which I approached Colombier. What tears of tenderness have I shed when on the road to it, while thinking of the paternal goodness, amiable virtues, and charming philosophy of this respectable old man! I called him father, and he called me son. These affectionate names give, in some measure, an idea of the attachment by which we were united, but by no means that of the want we felt of each other, nor of our continual desire to be together. He would absolutely give me an apartment at the castle of Colombier, and for a long time pressed me to take up my residence in that in which I lodged during my visits. I at length told him I was more free and at my ease in my own house, and that I had rather continue until the end of my life to come and see him. He approved of my candour, and never afterwards spoke to me on the subject. Oh, my good lord! Oh, my worthy father! How is my heart still moved when I think of your goodness? Ah, barbarous wretches! how deeply did they wound me when they deprived me of your friendship! But no, great man, you are and will ever be the same for me, who am still the same. You have been deceived, but you are not changed. My Lord Marechal is not without faults; he is a man of wisdom, but he is still a man. With the greatest penetration, the nicest discrimination, and the most profound knowledge of men, he sometimes suffers himself to be deceived, and never recovers his error. His temper is very singular and foreign to his general turn of mind. He seems to forget the people he sees every day, and thinks of them in a moment when they least expect it ; his attention seems ill-timed ; his presents are dictated by caprice and not by propriety. He gives or sends in an instant whatever comes into his head, be the value of it ever so small. A young Genevese, desirous of entering into the service of Prussia, made a personal application to him ; his lordship, instead of giving him a letter, gave him a little bag of peas, which he desired him to carry to the king. On receiving this singular recommendation his majesty gave a commission to the bearer of it. These elevated geniuses have between themselves a language which the vulgar will never understand. The whimsical manner of my Lord Marechal, something like the caprice of a fine woman, rendered him still more interesting to me. I was certain, and afterwards had proofs, that it had not the least influence over his sentiments, nor did it affect the cares prescribed by friendship on serious occasions, yet in his manner of obliging there is the same singularity as in his manners in general. Of this I will give one instance relative to a matter of no great importance. The journey from Motiers to Colombier being too long for me to perform in one day, I commonly divided it by setting off after dinner and sleeping at Brot, which is half way. The

landlord of the house where I stopt, named Sandoz, having
to solicit at Berlin a favour of importance to him, begged
I would request his excellency to ask it in his behalf.
Most willingly, said I, and took him with me. I left him
in the anti-chamber, and mentioned the matter to his lordship who returned me no answer. After passing with
him the whole morning, I saw as I crossed the hall to go
to dinner, poor Sandoz who was fatigued to death with
waiting. Thinking the governor had forgotten what I had
said to him, I again spoke of the business before we sat
down to table; but still received no answer. I thought
this manner of making me feel I was importunate rather
severe, and, pitying the poor man in waiting, held my
tongue. On my return the next day I was much surprised
at the thanks he returned me for the good dinner his
excellency had given him after receiving his paper. Three
weeks afterwards his lordship sent him the rescript he had
solicited, dispatched by the minister, and signed by the
king, and this without having said a word either to myself
or Sandoz concerning the business, about which I thought
he did not choose to give himself the least concern. I
could wish incessantly to speak of George Keith; from
him proceeds my recollection of the last happy moments I
have enjoyed; the rest of my life, since our separation, has
been passed in affliction and grief of heart. The remem-
brance of this is so melancholy and confused that it was
impossible for me to observe the least order in what I
write, so that in future I shall be under the necessity of
stating facts without giving them a regular arrangement.

I was soon relieved from my inquietude arising from the
uncertainty of my asylum, by the answer from his majesty
to the lord marshal, in whom, as it will readily be believed,
I had found an able advocate.   The king not only approved
of what he had done, but desired him, for I must relate
every thing, to give me twelve louis.   The good old man,
rather embarrassed by the commission, and not knowing
how to execute it properly, endeavoured to soften the insult
by transforming the money into provisions, and writing to
me that he had received orders to furnish me with wood
and coal to begin my little establishment ; he moreover
added, and perhaps from himself, that his majesty would
willingly build me a little house, such a one as I should
choose to have, provided I would fix upon the ground.   I
was extremely sensible of the kindness of the last offer,
which made me forget the weakness of the other."

This place the Earl left to be ambassador at the
court of Spain, a country to which he was extremely
partial.   While there, he became acquainted with the
family compact, then in process of formation, between the
two branches of the Bourbons, and is said to have sent
early notice of it to the then Prime Minister, the Earl of
Chatham.   Shortly after this, a Bill was brought into the
English Parliament, for the purpose of reversing the
attainder on the Earl ; and, on the 25th of May, 1759, it
was passed unanimously, so that he could now return to
Scotland and inherit property in Great Britain.   He,
therefore, made preparations to leave his embassy in Spain,
having received permission from Frederick to do so, and

had a farewell audience of the Spanish King on the 3d July, 1760. He immediately took his departure, and it was fortunate for him that he acted with such promptitude, for by it he escaped a very great danger, as within thirty-six hours of his departure from Madrid, notice was received there of the communication he had made to the Minister of England. On the 16th of August, in the same year, he was graciously received by George II., who, without doubt, was delighted to see the representative of the most powerful family in Scotland at his court, and taking the oath of allegiance to him. He seems, also, to have acted very generously towards him, presenting him to the right of a sum of £3618, which was yet unpaid by the parties who had purchased his estates, and offering him also his titles and honours. The latter he declined, feeling, no doubt, that, with the meagre pittance which he had, he would ill sustain the glory of a family that had once been the wealthiest in the country.

The reconciliation of the Earl to the House of Brunswick, and his taking the oath of allegiance (the oath to the Government was taken in the Court of King's Bench, 26th January, 1761) gave great umbrage to the remains of the Jacobite party that still existed in the country. In the district of Buchan, the feeling was very strong, and was given expression to in different ways. A very curious anecdote, to be found among the papers of Bishop Forbes, and said by him to have been related at his table by the celebrated Rev. John Skinner, author of "Tullochgorum," Episcopal Minister of Longside, illustrates the view of the

matter taken by the Jacobites of Buchan :—" It had been
a constant practice in the parish of Longside, in Aberdeenshire, to have bonfires, and even to ring the parish bell, on
the 2d of April, old style, the birthday of Earl Marischal.
On Thursday, the 12th February, being a general fast
throughout Scotland, when the bellman was ringing the
first bell, the news came to Longside containing the account
of the Earl Marischal's having taken the oaths at London ;
and that, at that very instant, the said bell rent from the
top downwards, and then across near the mouth, and that
soon after the bell had begun to ring. A gentleman
walking in his garden, about a quarter of a mile from the
church of Longside, asked a man passing by what the
matter was with the bell that it stopped so suddenly. The
answer being that she was rent, the gentleman said, 'Well,
do you know what the bell says by that ? even, Deil a
cheep mair sall I speak for you Earl Marischal.' "

On the 9th of September, we find him again in the
capital of his native land, after an absence of nearly half a
century. The Magistrates of Edinburgh, remembering
what his ancestors had done for their country, and his own
conscientious firmness when proclaiming the Pretender at
their ancient cross, determined to place his name in the roll
of her distinguished citizens. He then made a tour to the
north and west of Scotland, " and wherever his Lordship
went, his presence diffused such a joy as might naturally
be expected on the appearance of so worthy a representative
of so illustrious and ancient a family." About this time,
also, he succeeded to the estate of Kintore, which came to

him from a collateral branch of the family. He also
purchased back some of his estates, among which was the
land of St. Fergus, in which the Castle of Inverugie is
situated, for the sum of £12,620 10s., no one daring or
feeling inclined to bid against him ; but, when the trans-
action was finished, cheering like men mad with joy.

At Keithhall, he stayed for some time, feeling himself
by no means at home, as his habits of life, from long
residence in a foreign land, were altogether different from
those around him ; and the coldness of the climate greatly
affected his delicate constitution.   Besides this, he found
great difficulty in raising the money to pay the full price of
his estate, and began to get tired of the harassments
attendant upon such a state of matters.   Feeling greatly
the want of his old companions, he is said to have invited
Rousseau to come and spend the remainder of his days with
him at Inverugie.   He appears, at first, to have embraced
the offer ; but, before arrangements could be made, he
changed his mind.   Ere finally leaving the country, the
Earl determined to revisit the scenes of his youth, to gaze
upon those places around which he and his departed
brother had played in the careless, happy days of yore,
and to look again upon those towers, associated with
which were the sunniest and most sorrowful events in his
life.   To the Castle of Inverugie, therefore, he bent his
steps.

LAST VISIT TO INVERUGIE.

Notice of this had reached Peterhead, and everything in and around the little town wore a gay aspect. Preparations were made for a grand banquet in the Keith Mason Lodge, previous to which an address of welcome was to be read before the assembled multitude in Broad Street. When word was brought that the carriage was in sight, the town's folk formed in line, headed by the Magistrates, and marched out to meet their illustrious visitor. As soon as they came up to the carriage, he leaned forward, and scanned, with a careful eye, the vast crowd before him. Not one was known to him. At last, his eye lighted on Mr Forbes, one of his old companions. Instantly, a flash of recognition passed over his face, and he held out his hand. Forbes, stepping forward, shook it heartily ; and then, for a little, they could not speak, from the rush of memories which came upon them. Boys they were when last they met each other ; and now, after a separation of nearly fifty years, they stood side by side old men whose locks time had turned grey. To almost every question regarding their old companions, the Earl received the solemn word—Dead.

The carriage, accompanied by the Peterheadians and the farmers from St. Fergus, dressed in their Sunday clothes and mounted on horseback, moved slowly towards the town. When it was drawn up, and Mr Forbes had read the address of welcome, the immense crowd hurrahed and cheered in such a manner as Peterhead had never seen before. Deeply affected, the Earl stood in his carriage scarcely able to utter a word. A small incident, which took place at this very time, served to make the scene still more affecting. His old nurse, Mrs Gordon, bent with age and feeble in her step, pushed her way through the dense mass that surrounded the carriage, and made herself known to him. With an exclamation of surprise and joy, he bent down towards her, and took her thin hand in his. Into each others face they gazed with eyes blinded with tears, endeavouring to make out the features that were so well known more than half a century before. Kindly enquiring after her present welfare and comfort as far as he could in the presence of such a crowd, he shook into her hand, at parting, a sum of money, remarking that he was sorry it was not more, but that he was not now so rich as he once had been.

But a still more mournful duty was before him—the visit to Inverugie. Attended by an immense crowd, and escorted by the St. Fergus farmers as a guard of honour, he set out for the Castle. As he proceeded, the people gathered from every quarter to give him a hearty welcome and to testify their joy at his return. One old man, near the Collieburn, became so mad with joy that he set fire to his house for the purpose, he said, of making a bonfire in his honour, and threw some gold, with which he was to pay his rent, on the top of it, declaring that he " wid thack his hoose wi' gowd." Never did king or conqueror, from all classes of the community, meet with a more joyous welcome.

Near this place, he met one who had been a companion in many a day's ramble—Mr Fraser of Mains of Inverugie. He did not recognize him until he had heard his name, on which he grasped him warmly by the hand, and chatted about old times and the various places they passed. It took hours to reach Steadyvage, from which the first proper view of the Castle is obtained. As it came into sight, he gazed upon it as one does on the changed face of a friend in order that he may make out some feature by which he can recognise him. There it stood, roofless, tenantless ; its single black rafter lifting up its appealing form to the sky. For a few moments, he stood up in the carriage, with his eyes fixed on the old pile ; and then, summoning all his strength, he cried out, " Stop the stage ! stop the stage !" When this was done, he continued looking a little longer ; and then, throwing himself back, gave way to an agony of grief. All looked on in sympathy as the glory of his past was thus completely swept away, and his future rose up " all dark and barren as a rainy sea." Lifting his head, he took one longing, lingering look,—literally,

> Gazed and wept, gazed and wept, gazed and wept
> And gazed again,—

and then turned away for ever.

By a motion of the hand, for he could not trust himself to speak, he made known to the coachman that it was his wish to return. Slowly the cortege made its way back to Peterhead, and the turrets of Inverugie saw him no more.

Afterwards, sending his secretary to investigate the condition of the place, and finding it was completely in ruins, he gave up the idea of repairing it, and shortly after sold it to an ancestor of the present proprietor.

EARL MARISCHAL'S LAST DAYS.

Influenced by the urgent appeals of the King of Prussia, he decided to return to Berlin and spend the remainder of his days there.   One of the letters sent by the King to him when in this country presents him in such a pleasing light, and shows, so unmistakeably, his tender affection for the old Earl, that we cannot refrain from quoting it entire :—

"I cannot allow the Scotch the happiness of possessing you altogether.   Had I a fleet, I would make a descent on their coasts and carry you off.   The banks of the Elbe do not admit of these equipments; I must, therefore, have recourse to your friendship to bring you to him who esteems and loves you.   I loved your brother with my heart and soul ; I was indebted to him for great obligations. This is my right to you, this my title.

"I spend my time as formerly; only, at night, I read Virgil's Georgics, and go to my garden in the morning to make my gardener reduce them to practice.   He laughs both at Virgil and me, and thinks us both fools.

" Come to ease, to friendship, and philosophy ; these are what, after the battle of life, we must all have recourse to."

An anecdote, illustrative of his tender care for Lord Marischal, is given by the Earl of Buchan in one of his essays, and is worthy of being placed in comparison with

the famous story of his sleeping page.   It is to the following effect :—" One day at the Caffe, when the King was
in the midst of a most interesting conversation, he observed
old Lord Marischal of Scotland, who had been sick, fallen
asleep on a sofa in a corner of the room.   The King
immediately beckoned to the court for silence; and, treading
softly towards Lord Marischal, and taking out his pocket-
handkerchief, he threw it gently over the old man's head,
and retired into another apartment, where he took up the
conversation just where it had been interrupted."

A traveller, who visited Berlin in the year 1777, and
who had frequent opportunities of seeing the old Earl,
thus corroborates the fact of his familiar intimacy with the
King, and writes of him in the eighty-fifth year of his age,
about twelve months before his death :—" We dined
almost every day with the Lord Marischal, who was then
eighty-five years old, and was still as vigorous as ever both
in body and mind.   The King had given him a house
adjoining the gardens of Sans Souci, and frequently went
thither to see him.   He had excused himself from dining
with him, having found that his health would not allow
him to sit long at table ; and he was, of all those who had
enjoyed the favour of the King, the only one who could
truly be called his friend, and who was sincerely attached
to his person.   Of course, everybody paid court to him.
He was called the King's friend, and was the only one
who had merited that title, for he had always stood well
with him without flattering him."

In April, 1778, he was seized with fever ; and, after
suffering extreme pain for six weeks, died on the 28th of

May. During his illness, he never lost that sweetness of temper which was a marked characteristic in him, and often joked with his physician concerning his complaint and his end. On one occasion, he said to him, " I do not ask you to make me live ; for, apparently, you do not pretend to take fifty years off my age. I only beg you to shorten my sufferings, if it is possible. In fact, I have never been ill. I must have my share of the miseries of humanity, and I submit to that decree of nature."

Two days before he died, he sent for Mr Elliot, the English Minister at the court of Berlin, and said to him, in his usual cheerful and jocular manner, " I have asked you to come, because I find it pleasant that a Minister of King George should receive the last sighs of an old Jacobite. Moreover, you may perhaps have some commissions to give for my Lord Chatham (who had died a fortnight before) ; and, as I expect to see him to-morrow, or afterwards, I will take charge, with pleasure, of your despatches."

Thus passed away the last of the Marischals. He was a man of a most tender and affectionate heart ; of sound good sense, and so temperate in his judgments that his opinion was sought after by many. He was a master of conversation, and remarkable " for telling, with great point and brevity, an infinite number of very entertaining stories and anecdotes." Like his brother, he was a concise and elegant writer, a fact attributable to his early training. In the purity and accuracy of his writing, he forms a marked contrast to the majority of his contemporaries at the Pretender's court, and particularly his son, Charles Edward.

EARLY DIFFICULTIES.

JAMES KEITH we left making unsuccessful application to the Spanish Government for the renewal of his commission. On a change of Ministry, in 1721, he again brought the matter before them, but with no better success ; and, disgusted with this state of things, he asked permission and a passport to go to Italy. Having taken leave of all his friends, he set out for Barcelona, where he was agreeably surprised to find his commission awaiting him. Noticing, however, that it was a new one, and not a renewal of his old, he at once sent it back, declaring that he would accept of none but his former one. Instead, however, of proceeding to Italy, he returned to Madrid to see what would happen.

Next year, at the request of his mother, he determined to go to England to obtain possession of his patrimony, which had been confiscated along with his brother's estates. To prevent any misunderstanding on the matter, he called upon the English Minister at Madrid, and acquainted him with his intention. He strongly dissuaded him from it, assuring him that the Government were quite aware of the part he took in the attempt in 1719, and were at that time apprehensive of another. He advised him to go to Paris, and await a more settled state of things, which he did ; and, while there, word came that his affairs were satisfactorily arranged, and that there was, therefore, no need of his presence. By the aid of a female friend, he endeavoured, while in Paris, to get into the French service ; but, as he himself says, " by good luck it did not succeed," and so he remained there during the whole of 1723 and 1724.

When the marriage between the King of France and the Infanta of Spain was broken off in the year 1725, all the Spanish officers were ordered to return to their country. Though he could not properly be considered one, his nice sense of honour induced him to follow in the train of the Infanta. Arrived there, he found the country in an extra-ordinary state of excitement and exasperation at everything French, and a war every moment imminent. After a little, matters cooled down, and the adventurer had to retire to Valentia, disappointed in an opportunity of proving his courage and ability.

In the following year, an attempt being made on Gibraltar, he again requested to be employed in the expedition. To this he received the usual answer— " That, being a Protestant, the king could not give me any command in his troops ; on which I asked the per-mission to serve the campaign as a volunteer, fully resolved it should be the last I should make in that country, where

I saw that only mere necessity to be revenged on the
English had made them take me into their service, and
where I must pass the rest of my life, not only without
advancement, but even without exercising the employment
I had.   However, I resolved to pass the campaign without
complaining, and then take my party." Through the
whole, therefore, of this strange and ridiculous campaign
he served uncomplainingly, as he did many a time afterwards before he attained to his distinguished rank of
Field-Marshal.   After a seige of five months, and the loss
of 2000 men, the Spaniards were compelled to acknowledge
that the place was impregnable.   However, according to
the showing of Keith, the place was so carelessly guarded,
and their men allowed to enter and leave without being
searched, that, if the leader of the Spaniards had pleased,
he might have taken the place by a surprise.   Such an
idea seems never to have entered his head, and our world-
renowned fortress remained permanently in our hands.

Before finally leaving, he made a last application for
employment in the service of Spain, through the king's
confessor.   Having stated his time of service, the fact that
he was now the oldest colonel of the British nation, and
the hope that he would be promoted to the first Irish
regiment vacant, he patiently waited a reply.   It came in
the usual terms ; and, though he must by this time have
been reduced in circumstances, and the reply of the king
—"that, how soon he knew I was a Roman Catholic, I
should not only have what I asked, but that he would
take care of my fortune"—very tempting, and such as few

would have resisted, yet we find him preferring poverty to riches, honour to dishonour, the faith of his youth to the tenets of Rome, and, at the age of 32, setting out to begin the world afresh in a country entirely new to him, and among a people of whose language he did not know a single word.

There is no doubt that the success of his countryman, Patrick Gordon, at the court of Russia, must have weighed very much with him in the choice of country. In the district of Buchan, of which he was a native, his fame must have been well known ; and, being connected with the Gordon family, he must have often been the subject of conversation at the table of Earl Marischal. That young Keith had this country in view long before this time, we have ample proof from his autobiography ; for, in the year 1717, when only 20 years of age, and when he thought it high time to be doing something for himself, on the occasion of a visit of Peter the Great to Paris, he endeavoured to get into his service, but, as he himself says, " the attempt did not succeed, perhaps because I did not take the right means to it."

RUSSIAN SERVICE.

Through the influence of his friend the Duke of Liria, who was Spanish ambassador at the court of Russia, he was appointed a major-general in the army of Peter the Second. Leaving Spain, after receiving an honorarium of

1000 crowns from the king, he went by way of Paris,
Flanders, and Holland, and embarked at Amsterdam for
St. Petersburg.   Arrived there, he wrote to the Duke of
Liria, who advised him to come at once to Moscow, where
the court then was ; but, being fatigued with his journey,
he staid sometime at Cronstadt, and arrived at the old
capital when the king was gone on a hunting expedition.
After paying court to all the men of rank to whom the
Duke had introduced him, he was presented to the king ;
and, a few days afterwards, received orders from the
Field-Marshal Prince Dolgoruski to take the command of
two regiments of foot in quarters near Moscow.   This,
however, he did not undertake, as he was entirely un-
acquainted with the language, but devoted himself so
assiduously to its acquirement that, in the space of three
months, he was able to take the command and perform
thoroughly the duties of an officer.

On the death of the Emperor and accession of Anne,
the Dolgoruski, who governed the country under the late
Emperor, were deprived of all power and banished to
Siberia.   The oath of allegiance formed by Peter the Great
was ordered to be taken by all her subjects ; and, when a
settlement had been made, she proceeded to reward those
who had faithfully served and stood by her in her past and
present condition.   Among these was Keith, who, though
he had only been one year in the country, and was by no
means looking for advancement, was raised to one of the
most important posts in the empire.   As this story illustrates the insecure existence of the generals and officials at

the Russian court, we will give it in his own words :—
" One evening I was surprised to receive a billet from
Lieutenant-General le Fort, advertising me that the Count
Levenwolde desired I should come to court next day, he
having something to communicate to me. I reaved all
night what could be the meaning of such a message ; I
consulted myself if I had done anything amiss which might
demand a reprimand from the Empress by her adjutant,
and finding myself entirely innocent, I concluded I might
have some enemy at court who might misrepresent me.
Full of these thoughts, I went next morning to Lieutenant-
General le Fort, whom I found with his cousin the Polish
Envoyé and the Duke of Liria. My first question was, if
Count Levenwolde had told him nothing of what he had
to say to me, or if he had discovered nothing in his face
that marked his being displeased with me. He assured me
no, and that he told him nothing of what he had to say.
The Duke of Liria, who was present, and who saw my
embaras, said that he was informed that the regiment
which was raising for Count Levenwolde was to be guards,
and that perhaps he designed to propose me as a lieutenant-
colonel ; to which I answered that it was already published
in the army as an ordinary regiment, with the difference of
a battalion more, in which case I could not accept the
lieutenant-colonel, and if it was a regiment of guards, I
was pretty sure the employment would not be proposed to
me (being commonly filled by generals-in-chief or lieutenant-
generals), who was one of the youngest major-generals of
the army. Every one agreed with me that it must be

something else, and in this doubt I arrived at Ismailof, where the court then was, and where I made my reverence to Count Levenwolde, *d' un air tres embarassé*. How soon he saw me, he took me aside, and after a compliment which entirely assured me, he proposed me the lieutenant-colonel of his regiment, which was to be guards ; and at the same time told me that I might take twenty-four hours to consult if I would accept it. I thanked him immediately for the preference he had given me over so many who deserved such a trust better, and for the twenty-four hours they were needless, since I accepted the honour in the instant ; and two days after he presented me to the Empress, who declared me lieutenant-colonel of her guards. All Moscow was as surprised as I was myself; and as the employment is looked on as one of the greatest trust in the empire, and that the officers of the guards are regarded as domestics of the sovereign, I received hundreds of visits from people I had never seen nor heard of in my life, and who imagined that certainly I must be in great favour at court, in which they were prodigiously deceived."

In the gay court of Anne, Keith played the part of the courtier ; and, having had the good fortune to mingle with the aristocracy of the most famous and civilized countries in Europe, he must have been looked up to as an authority on all matters of etiquette, of which the Russian court had been as yet singularly destitute. Under Peter the Great, the court devoted its attention more to matters affecting war and the state, and considered courtly manners beneath their notice ; while, during the reign of Catherine, so little order or regularity was kept that it did not seem like a court at all. Peter the Second rather helped to increase than diminish the notion which was prevalent in the other courts of Europe, that the Russian nation was barbarous and uncourtly, and to Anne was left the task of undoing this. It is said that, in five years, she did more to civilize the court and make it respected in Europe than Peter did during the whole of his reign. Around her she collected ambassadors from the most powerful and ancient kingdoms both of Europe and Asia, so that Moscow appeared liker a city composed of men from various nations, than like the capital of one great empire. Among these Keith mingled with the courtly ease of one who felt himself at home in their company, and equal, if not superior, to most of them both in mind and manners.

In the year 1732, Keith was appointed inspector-general of the department bordering on the frontier of Asia, along the rivers Volga and Don, with a part of the frontier of Poland, about Smolensko. Leaving Moscow, where it must not be forgotten that he had been left in full command of the troops during the temporary absence of the Empress at St. Petersburg, he went, in the month of June, to his province, where he passed in review all the regiments to the number of thirty-two, and travelled during that circuit no fewer than 1500 leagues. In the beginning of the next year, he returned to St. Petersburg to make his report to the Empress and the College of War, when he found the court in a state of great excitement occasioned by the death of the king of Poland. Russia, after some hesitation, espoused the cause of Augustus, son of the deceased king, in opposition to Stanislaus, who had been elected by a majority of the nation, or of the nobles who exercised the right of king-making. Owing, however, to discussions among the people and the march of General Lacy on the capital, he was compelled to retire to Dantzic, where he was besieged by a confederate army of Russians, Saxons, and Poles; and, after a long and heroic defence, was compelled to flee. As an instance of the fierceness of the contest before the city, it may be mentioned that in one assault alone 8000 of the Russian troops are said to have fallen. Keith, who had been ordered from his province to assist Lacy, entered Poland with six battalions of foot, 600 dragoons, and 4000 Cossacks. Marching through the country, conquering all before him or drawing them over to his side, he at last arrived at Dantzic, and took a very active part in the siege. For his distinguished services on this occasion, he was raised to the rank of lieutenant-general.

During this and subsequent campaigns, Keith saw, with detestation and disgust, the barbarous manner in which the Russians conducted the operations of war. Unlike any other civilized nation, they invariably destroyed the country through which they passed, pillaging, burning, and killing all that came in their way, so that the very name of the Russians was dreaded and execrated. Having been sent on one of those raiding expeditions, he endeavoured to excuse himself; but, when he was positively refused, and commanded to do his duty, he set out, determined to teach them a lesson in warfare. Instead, therefore, of destroying and burning all before him, he collected the cattle and horses and sent them to the army, at the same time informing his commander that, if the country continued to be ravaged in this manner, it would quickly become a desert, and they themselves soon die of hunger. Moved by this threat, and perhaps aware that his officer was in reality disregarding his orders, he recalled him, and Keith had the satisfaction of knowing that he had boldly set his face against unnecessary cruelty, and shamed a barbarous leader into something like humanity.

After this came a war with the Turks, because they had paid no attention to the continued complaints of Russia regarding the incursions of the Tartars. Munnich, the chief in command, attacked the town of Azoff; but, as the Tartars advanced to its relief, he left the siege to another of his generals, and went to meet them. Having defeated them and advanced into Crim Tartary, carrying everything before him, he returned to the Ukraine, put his troops into winter quarters along the Dneiper, and went to St. Petersburg. Before doing so, however, he appointed Keith to the chief command of all the Russian forces in the Ukraine. This was such a mark of confidence in his abilities and prudence as to unmistakeably show the estimate in which he held him. Steadily was he rising in the scale of importance; and the masterly manner in which he protected his troops from the continual attacks of the Turks and Tartars, and the splendid condition in which the commander-in-chief found them on his arrival in March, still more increased his confidence in him.

During this campaign, Munnich, with Keith as second in command, laid siege to Ockzakow, a strong Turkish town between the Black Sea and the estuary of the Dneiper. His siege train and stores of every sort had been sent off in full time to reach the place, but had been detained by a number of unforeseen accidents. What artillery he had, he managed to plant in a deserted garden, and for two days blazed away at the town. On the second, some wooden houses in the town were set on fire, and the flames spread with alarming rapidity. During the disturbance caused by this, Munnich determined to make an attack on the place, and, if possible, carry it by an escalade. " 'Advance within musket shot, General Keith,' orders Munnich's aide-de-camp, cantering up. 'I have been this good while within it,' answers Keith, pointing to his dead men. Aide-de-camp canters up a second time, ' Advance within half-musket shot, General Keith, and quit any covert you have.' Keith does so ; sends with his respects to Field-Marshal Munnich his remonstrance against such a waste of human life. Aide-de-camp canters up a third time, ' Field-Marshal Munnich is for trying a scalade ; hopes General Keith will do his best to co-operate.' ' Forward, then !' answers Keith ; advances close to the glacis ; finds a wet ditch twelve feet broad, and has not a stitch of engineer furniture. Keith waits there two hours ; his men under fire all the while trying this and that to get across ; Munnich's scalade going off ineffectual in like manner ;—till, at length, Keith's men tire, and all men tire of such a business, and roll back in great confusion out of

shot range." Such was the sort of work Keith had
to go through and endure—a recklessness displayed in
every movement, a useless expenditure of human life,
and an utter disregard of the very means by which
every careful and consummate general paves his way to
victory.

During this war with Turkey a very curious incident
happened to Keith, illustrative of the " wandering Scot."
In the year 1739, when a treaty of peace was being agreed
upon between the two belligerents, the commissioners for
this purpose were Keith on the part of Russia, and the Grand
Vizier on that of Turkey. These two personages met
and carried on their negotiations by means of interpreters.
When all was concluded they rose to separate. Keith
made his bow with his hat in his hand, and the Vizier his
salaam with his turban on his head. But, when these
were over, the Vizier turned suddenly round, and, coming
up to Keith, took him by the hand, declaring in the
broadest Scotch dialect that it made him " unco happy to
meet a countryman in his exalted station." Keith, completely surprised, looked eagerly for an explanation, when
the Vizier said, " Dinna be surprised, man ; I'm o' the
same country wi' yoursel'. I min weel seein' you and yer
brither, when boys, passin'. My father, sir, was *bellman
o' Kirkcaldy*."

It was at the seige of Ockzakow that he received the
wound in the knee already referred to, and which afterwards gave him so much trouble. By it he was recognised
on the field of Hochkirchen, when stripped by the Croats,

E

by that General Lascy at whose side he had so often fought
in battle when in the Russian service.

While in France, as we have already mentioned when
treating of his brother, he was entrusted with some diplomatic matters regarding the war then going on between
Sweden and Russia.   He also was commissioned to repair
to England to manage some matters of very great moment.
He arrived in London in February, 1740, and on the 15th
of that month was presented to his majesty George II.,
who received him most graciously.   The rebel of 1715
and 1719 was entirely forgotten, and he was looked upon
as a great general, and the plenipotentiary of one of the
greatest empires of Europe.   On the 14th of May he received his audience of leave, but remained in London four
days longer.

It was during his visit to this country that the Magistrates of Peterhead sent to him a letter of congratulation
on his return to England.   It was dated the 23d February,
but no answer was received until the month of June,
owing to the press of public business, and the numerous
invitations showered upon him both by his own friends
and by the greatest men of the day.   The reply was
written in London, but was sent from Elsinore under cover
to John Keith, with orders to forward it to the Magistrates
of Peterhead.   This person, a relation of the General's,
says, in an accompanying letter, that he " had the honour
of drinking all their healths (the Magistrates of Peterhead)
with Lord Kintore and his Excellency (General Keith),
who expresses a particular regard to his native country,

and particularly to the good town of Peterhead. The General's reply is to the following effect :—

"GENTLEMEN,

"I received with the greatest pleasure the letter you did me the honour to write me, and return you my most sincere thanks for your kind wishes and expressions in regard to myself and family; nothing could be more agreeable to me than to see that, after so long an absence, I am still remembered by my countrymen, and particularly by those whom I'm obliged to look on as nearer to me than even most of the rest. I am only sorry that my gratitude can be but expressed at present in words, but I hope you will be persuaded, that in everything that lyes in my power, nobody will be readier and willinger to serve you than,

"GENTLEMEN,

"Your most obedient and most humble servant,

"JAMES KEITH."

"London, May 4, 1740."

While absent on this affair of state, peace was concluded between the Turks and the Russians, on which occasion St. Petersburg was the scene of great rejoicings. All the officers who had been engaged in the war were handsomely rewarded by the Empress ; and Keith, though absent, was not forgotten. He received a gold-hilted sword worth £1500, and was made governor of the whole Ukrane, to which province he repaired in the month of July.

In October of this year, the Empress Anne died, and the Emperor Iwan succeeded, the administration of affairs being, however, entirely vested in the hands of Biron, his tutor. Keith, willing to acknowledge the Emperor, refused to have anything to do with the man whom he had

E 2

placed at the head of the government.   In this peculiar
position, with full power over a people devoted to him,
both from the mildness of his rule and the justice of his
administration, he continued for twenty-two days, when
the authority of Biron ended.   And it was, perhaps, well
that it did so; for, had it come to an open rupture, the
nation would have found great difficulty in quelling a
rebellion headed by such a leader, and with troops so
devoted to him as those of the Ukrane were.   The mother
of the Emperor having undertaken the government of the
country, confirmed Keith in all his offices.

A war with Sweden having arisen, Field-Marshal
Lascy, with Keith as second in command, was sent against
them, and appeared before Wybourg at the head of 50,000
men.   A variety of bloody engagements took place, and in
almost every one of them the Russians were victorious.
The first of these took place on September 3, near
Williamstrand, when the Russians gained a decided
triumph, the town being carried sword in hand, and 3000
Swedes either killed or taken prisoners, among the latter
being the Swedish Major-General Wrangel, who headed
the detachment.   Keith was very much admired and
praised for his gallant conduct during the whole of this
campaign, and a substantial mark of the favour of the
court was given him in the augmentation of his income.
But what must have been still more gratifying to him was
the fact of Lascy, on his departure for St Petersburg, after
the reduction of Williamstrand and the return to Wybourg,
leaving him in full command of the army before that city,

with other two generals of great note under him, more especially when the whole Swedish forces were said to be in full march to raise the seige.

Meantime, a revolution in St. Petersburg elevated Elizabeth, daughter of Peter the Great, to the throne; and Keith, following the example of Lascy, took the oath of allegiance. Not long after her accession, a truce was agreed upon between Sweden and Russia, for the purpose of bringing about a peace. Finding, however, the demands of Sweden too high, hostilities were resumed, and the Swedes, pursued beyond the river Kymen, were compelled to abandon their stores and provisions. In quick succession, Nyslot, Helsingfors, and Abo, the capital of Finland, were surrendered; and, in a few months, the whole province fell into the hands of the Russians. Besides the loss of this fine tract of country, Sweden had the mortification to discover that her national spirit was gone; that her once brave and hardy troops no longer maintained their superiority in the field; and that their former opponents, whom they had despised as undisciplined barbarians, were now become their masters in that very art which, but a few years before, made them the terror and admiration of all Christendom. This result, which seems to have so much surprised the Swedes, was mainly owing to the strenuous and untiring exertions of Lascy, Keith, and the various other foreign generals who had been imported into the Russian army. And yet their position was anything but a comfortable one, for they were assailed on every side by the mean jealousies of the other Russian leaders, and made to feel, with acute bitterness, the fact of their being foreigners and adventurers. Their number and high position prevented any open quarrel; but, nevertheless, they were gradually looking forward to the time when they would be able to free themselves from this splendid slavery. Accordingly, at this time, the whole of them requested permission to retire. Keith was among the number, and some very strong reason must have induced him to do so, for none had been treated with greater kindness and honour, and was held in higher esteem. The Empress, afraid of losing one of her best generals, did everything in her power to retain him, giving him the Order of St. Andrew, and offering him the chief command against the Persians. The former he accepted, but the latter he declined, consenting to remain in her service, and so influencing the others that they all followed his example.

The Swedish queen having died, the succession to the throne gave rise to great difficulties and the interference of Russia. Keith, being sent against them, seized the island of Aland, and, with a fleet under his command, fought a bloody engagement with the Swedes, greatly annoying them with a battery which he had caused to be planted on the shore, and only ceasing the battle when it had continued far into the night, and the Swedish fleet had retired. Negotiations having been entered into, the Empress offered to restore to the Swedes a great part of their conquests, on condition of their electing Duke Adolphus Frederick of Holstein, and Bishop of Lubeck, as their king. The evident advantages that would necessarily flow from this arrangement bore down all opposition, and the prince was declared hereditary king of Sweden.

The Swedish peasentry being dissatisfied with this arrangement, and anxious for the elevation of the Prince of Denmark to the throne, sought to gratify their rage by demanding vengeance on the leaders of the forces in Finland. These, without any real proofs of guilt, were condemned to death, and after a time suffered the extreme penalty of the law. To some extent soothed by this disgraceful act of injustice, they yielded their consent to the election of Duke Adolphus, and greeted him on his arrival at Stockholm with the most extravagant demonstrations of joy. The Dalcarlians, however, excited by the Danes, rose in arms to the number of 20,000, and marched to the capital demanding the abdication of the Duke. He, unwilling to proceed to extreme measures, tried every method to appease them ; and, finding these useless, called out the military and endeavoured to put it down by force. A fierce contest took place in the midst of the city, in which 3000 of the rebels were slain and the rest obliged to surrender. Fearing, however, that the influence of Denmark would again cause a revolt, the King solicited the aid of Russia, and Keith was sent with 10,000 men to overawe the people. He arrived in October before Stockholm, and was received by the King with the greatest distinction. The terror of his name, and the memory of his recent prowess both by land and sea, seem to have produced the most beneficial results. Besides being commander-in-chief, he also acted as minister plenipotentiary for his sovereign, and in this latter capacity commanded

the respect of his enemies. His integrity, hatred of
double-dealing, and plain speaking when he discovered
any attempts of this nature on the part of the Swedes,
gained him the confidence not only of the King but also of
the people.   The former, along with the prince-successor,
rivaled each other in testifying the high esteem in which
they held him.   On New-year's-day the monarch presented
him with a splendid sword ; and, when he had his audience
of leave on the 23d June, he received another, together
with the portrait of the prince-successor and £1000 in
money.   When he returned to Russia, the Empress received him most graciously, being proud of a general and
ambassador who was "alike successful in conducting the
operations of war and negotiations for peace."

It was during this war with Sweden that Keith displayed an instance of most remarkable personal courage,
which ought not to pass unnoticed.   The Russian soldiers,
having become enraged at a letter brought by a Swedish
trumpeter to an officer in the Russian service, cried out
that they were betrayed, rushed like madmen to the tents
of the foreign officers and dragged them forth, intending
to murder them.   Keith, on hearing the noise, ran from
his tent, walked direct into the heart of the infuriated mob,
seized the ringleader by the collar of the coat, sent for the
confessor and the hangman, and ordered the fellow to
instant execution.   By this bold and prompt action he
completely quelled the mutiny ; and, had not Marshal
Lascy come and by concert pardoned him, the mutineer
would most certainly have been executed.

In 1745 Keith had to give his personal help to the

King of Poland, menaced by the King of Prussia ; but, after the battle of Kesselsdorf and the taking of Dresden, the war came to an end. Next year, Elizabeth, with all her court, went in great state into the district of Livonia, where Keith was stationed, and reviewed the troops with him at their head.

Before leaving this part of his history we may mention a circumstance which, if it can be relied on, is, to say the least, most remarkable. It may have been noticed by the reader that the Empress Elizabeth showed on every occasion particular favour to Keith. It has been said, on what evidence we cannot at present exactly define, that she fell in love with Keith, offered to marry him, and of course raise him to the highest dignity in the state. He had the good sense, says the same authority, to refuse the dangerous honour, and soon after left the Russian service. That she had a strong affection for him is borne out by facts, for we find her, after his departure, earnestly requesting him to correspond with her ; and in one of her letters letting fall the remarkable expression, " Your letters are health and happiness to me." And, to say the least of it, the alliance would have been no disgrace to her, and it would have materially strengthened her position on the throne. He could boast of a lineage far more ancient and famous than she, and he was in himself the only general of the Russians who could, from his personal influence with the soldiers, and his firm, indomitable courage, sway the sceptre with a hand worthy of the husband of a daughter of Peter the Great.

This may have been one of the causes which induced him to leave the Russian service, though we have other and more cogent ones. It seems that there had been a great deal of intriguing and underhand dealing among the Russian officials with reference to the chief command of the army, all done with the real view of keeping Keith from the post, which was his due both from age and length of service. The preference of a Russian much his junior filled up the measure of his disgust, which was still more increased by the fact of the Government refusing to engage his brother, the Earl, who had come to visit him. He, therefore, left the country where his services had been at last so badly requited, and made his way to Hamburg.

PRUSSIAN SERVICE.

Our soldier of fortune, on arriving at Hamburg, wrote to Frederick the Great, offering his sword, which that king, having been watching of late years the way in which he had been acting, and knowing his real value, immediately accepted, and at once made him field-marshal, with an income of £1200 a year. The letter was dated the 1st September, 1747, and his appointment of field-marshal the 15th September following. Two years later, he added the dignity of Governor of Berlin, and invested him with the Order of the Black Eagle. His income at this time was £2400, exclusive of emoluments and gratifications which he received from time to time.

Four days after his arrival, he indited a letter to his brother, which shows such clearness of mental vision and such correct observation, that we do not scruple to give it entire :—

"I have now the honour, and which is still more, the pleasure of being with the king at Potsdam, where he ordered me to come 17th curt., two days after he declared me field-marshal, where I have the honour to dine and sup with him every day. He has more wit than I have wit to tell you; speaks solidly and knowingly on all kinds of subjects; and I am much mistaken if, with the experience of four campaigns, he is not the best officer of his army. He has several persons—Rothenburg, Winterfeld, Swedish Rudenskjold (just about departing), not to speak of D'Argens and the French— with whom he lives in almost the familiarity of a friend, but has no favourite, and shows a natural politeness for everybody who is about him. For one who has been four days about his person, you will say I pretend to know a great deal of his character; but what I tell you, you may depend upon. With more time, I shall know as much of him as he will let me know—and all his ministry knows no more."

From this it may be seen that Keith considered Frederick the beau-ideal of a warrior, and looked up to him as the great soldier of the age.

For nine years after his arrival in Prussia, he enjoyed the sweets of peace to which he had been so long a stranger, and acquired honour to himself in the departments of arts and belles-lettres. His active mind was never at rest, but always engaged on subjects often very dissimilar. He was the king's art collector—his picture buyer,—and seems to have conducted this peculiar business as much to his satisfaction as he afterwards did many a

battle and seige. He also prepared plans for bridges over
the river Spree; endeavoured, by every means in his
power, to open up the East Indian trade to Prussian
industry; and tried to induce the king to allow English
woollen manufacturers to settle in the country. The
Royal Academy, proud of having a governor alike remarkable for his military genius and his literary acquirements,
enrolled his name in the list of their honorary members,
and considered that glory was reflected upon them rather
than upon him by such an action.

Notwithstanding his large income, Keith, who was
particularly liberal in money matters, often by his generosity
exceeded the income allowed him; and, knowing that
Frederick visited such conduct with his displeasure, he, as
the less of two evils, at such times absented himself from
court. Frederick, on one of these occasions, requiring to
see him on some business of importance, called at his
house, and found the marshal in his garden employed in
pointing paper cannons at pins of wood, and noting how
he might pour the greatest quantity of fire upon them as
their position changed. Learning the cause of his absence,
the king cheerfully paid his debts, entered with the greatest
of pleasure into his amusement, caused the number of pins
to be increased to many thousands, and had often many a
keen engagement in the garden, which was of great service
to them afterwards in the field. The marshal also in-
vented an amusement in imitation of the game of chess, at
which the king and he used to play. Having caused
several thousands of small statues of men in armour to be

cast, he set them opposite to each other, ranged them in battalions as if he had been drawing up an army; and, by bringing out some of the wings or centre, showed the advantage or disadvantage resulting from the different draughts which were made.

During these quiet years, he seems to have been growing in favour with all classes, but particularly with the king. Listen to the words of Carlyle, who potographs him with a distinctness that almost makes us see the real man :—" A man of Scotch type; the broad accent, with its sagacities, veracities, with its stedfastly fixed moderation and its sly twinkles of defensive humour, is still audible to us through the foreign wrappings. Not given to talk unless there is something to be said, but well capable of it then. Frederick, the more he knows him, likes him the better. On all manner of subjects he can talk knowingly, and with insight of his own. On Russian matters Frederick likes especially to hear him, though they differ in regard to the worth of Russian troops. . . . Frederick greatly respects the sagacious gentleman with the broad accent."

But the seven years' war began, and Keith was ushered again into the turmoil of a contest, one of the most remarkable of modern times. Marching into Saxony—which Frederick was compelled to do from the fear that he was to be stripped of Silesia by the allied confederation of France, Austria, Saxony, and Russia,—the king, along with Keith as first in command under him, met the Austrians at Lowositz. There was fought the first battle of this war; and in it Keith displayed the same military genius which had formerly rendered him famous.   By the side of the king, in the very thick of the battle, was his tall and commanding figure to be seen encouraging his men both by words and gestures.   In the following year, the Prussians, having penetrated into Bohemia, engaged and defeated the Austrains in front of the city of Prague ; and, after they had retreated into it, laid seige to the place. From the post where the marshal was stationed, the severest attacks were made ; and it was, no doubt, on this account that the enemy determined to surprise him, by sallying out and making an attack on his lines in the dead of the night.   But they reckoned beyond their host ; for, as soon as the first shot was fired, Keith was on horseback giving orders, and, in fifteen minutes, had his troops ready to receive them.   On came the Austrians mad with brandy, and furious to revenge themselves on their late victors. The first line received them bravely, and, despite their reiterated attacks, kept them back until the arrival of reinforcements.   For two hours, this unequal and desperate contest had been going on in the grim darkness, when Keith, pushing his way to the front, charged at the head of his men, and drove back the Austrians with a loss of 1000 killed and wounded.   Again, four days after, they made another sally, and were received as hotly, and driven back as furiously, as before.   The king, who was on the other side of the river, and therefore not able to assist in the battle, wrote next morning to the marshal with great glee :—" My dear Field-Marshal,—The night of the 23d will prove as decisive as the day of the 6th.   I thank heaven for the advantages you have gained over the enemy —above all, for the slight loss we have sustained." The smallness of the loss seems to have been of almost as great importance to him as the victory, for he afterwards refers to it in a postscript with evident pleasure. And to one who, like Frederick, had great difficulty in obtaining troops, and who guarded carefully each individual soldier, this was indeed a very great consideration. From this, it may be seen that the prodigality of the Russians regarding men had had no bad effect on Keith ; for, even in this very imminent danger, he had protected his men so carefully that his loss was extremely small.

The seige of Prague having been abandoned, Keith was commissioned to retreat and join the king. This he did without the loss of a man, though the enemy was continually hanging on his rear, and doing everything in their power to impede his march. With an army of 16,000 he left Bohemia, after drawing from that kingdom the supplies necessary for their support, and, marching through Saxony, joined the king at Bautzen. Thus, in the most disagreeable of all duties to a soldier and general—retreat,—Keith showed himself not only ready to obey, but also able to perform in the most masterly manner.

Having come to the conclusion that now was the time to crush Frederick, his enemies determined to make a simultaneous attack upon him, and thus, by dividing his forces, complete his ruin. The French, under Soubize, marched on Saxony, where Keith was stationed ; Richielieu was kept in awe by a force under Prince Ferdinand of

Brunswick, and Haddock by another under Prince Maurice. Haddock, however, eluding the Prince, marched at once on Berlin ; and the king, hearing of this when encamped at Naumburg, rushed with a very small army to save his own dominions. Thus, a mere handful of soldiers—in fact, less than 4000 men—were left under the command of Keith to oppose Soubize. His enemies knew this, and joked very heartily about the "army" they were about to attack. Arrived with a very superior force at Leipsic, into which Keith had been forced, they at once demanded a surrender, but Keith sent back word that he intended to defend the place to the last, adding the following noble words :—"Tell the Prince of Hildburghausen (the commander of the enemy's forces) that by birth I am a Scotchman, by choice and duty a Prussian ; and I am determined so to defend the town that neither the Scotch nor the Prussians shall be ashamed of me. The king, my master, has commanded me to keep the place, and I shall keep it." On a second summons being sent, accompanied with permission to the Prussians to leave the town unhindered, and Keith rejecting it with scorn, the Prince was enraged, and declared that he would lay Berlin and Potsdam in ashes. Keith only laughed at the threat, and proceeded quietly with the formation of his trenches and ramparts. After some little time, a note came from the king to the following effect :—"Be easy ; the Prince of Hildburghausen will not eat you ; I will answer for it." To this Keith replied, "I have just received the letter in which your Majesty tells me that you are going to bring me powder, artillery, and everything needful. When I have that, he who wishes to eat me will perhaps find me a very tough morsel." Having received some reinforcement, he again advanced, and joined the king at Rossbach. Two days afterwards, the Prussians gained the most famous victory that was obtained through the whole war. The battle lasted for an hour and a half, and ended in a total defeat to the enemy—18,000 men beating 60,000. Here Keith eminently distinguished himself, and very materially helped to the success of the battle.

Shortly after this victory, Frederick marched into Silesia with inconceivable rapidity, and defeated the Austrians in the battle of Lissa or Leuthen as signally as he had done the French at Rossbach. With only 33,000 men, he engaged the Austrians under Prince Charles of Lorraine at the head of 92,000 men, and completely defeated him with the loss of 7000 men, 21,500 prisoners, and 134 pieces of artillery, while he himself only lost 3000 killed and wounded. By this victory, he recovered the towns of Breslau and Lignitz, and the greater part of Silesia. Keith, during this time, was busy in another direction. Setting out for the magazine of Leitmeritz, he took it, having, by forced marches, arrived there one day before General Marshal who had flown to save it. The city of Prague, remembering the last time when he was before her walls, only a few months before, trembled for the consequences, and made active preparations for his reception. But it was too far into the season to think of a siege, and so Keith returned into Saxony, and arrived

without the loss of a man at Chemnitz, on the very day
on which Frederick gained the battle of Lissa.

The campaign of 1758 was commenced in the month
of March.   Quitting Breslau, the king joined his army
then occupying the mountains lying between Silesia and
Bohemia.   Schweidnitz, a strongly fortified town about
30 miles from Breslau, was attacked and taken about the
middle of April, after which the whole Prussian army was
concentrated near the town of Landshut.   Keith was
ordered to besiege Olmutz, the chief fortress of Moravia,
situated on an island in the river.   This he did, but without
success ; for a series of untoward accidents prevented him
from prosecuting the siege with his accustomed vigour.
He was, therefore, compelled to raze it, which operation
he performed with complete success.   During the retreat,
he was engaged in several severe engagements with the
enemy, in all of which he behaved with such courage and
watchfulness that the retreat of the besieging corps from
Olmutz is considered one of the most splendid on record.
At last, he arrived at Koniggratz, a town and fortress of
Bohemia rather more than 60 miles from Prague ; and,
taking the place, continued there till the beginning of
August, when Frederick began to direct his operations
against the Russians ; but the marshal was prevented, by
sickness, from accompanying him.

THE BATTLE OF HOCHKIRCHEN.

When scarcely recovered from his illness, Keith went to Breslau to join the king, who was making preparations for opposing Marshal Daun, the Austrian leader. Entrusted with a grand convoy to the king's army, he had reached the village of Hochkirch or Hochkirchen, half way between Bautzen and Lobau. Here he found that Frederick, with 30,000 troops, had taken up an almost untenable position, which was rendered still more precarious from the proximity of Daun, with a force of 50,000 Austrians. Keith warned him of the danger to which he was exposed by the vicinity of the enemy and the nature of the ground; but Frederick, despising the enemy, would listen to no remonstrance.

About five in the morning of the 14th October, under cover of a thick fog, Daun, who had been watching his opportunity, surprised the Prussian camp. The roar of the cannon told Keith that the enemy were upon them, that what he had dreaded and earnestly warned the king against was at last come. Mounting his horse, he rushed to the scene of action, and, by his word and presence, endeavoured to encourage his men. Thrice, during the grim, murky darkness of that foggy morning, did the efforts of this brave man drive back the Austrians; but the superiority of their number and the suddenness of their surprise were very much in their favour. Considering that his presence in the front would assist very materially to the success of his men, as in a similar surprise before Prague, he rushed into the very thick of the battle, and, by the conspicuous part he acted, drew upon him the notice of the enemy.   Believing that his death would be the utter defeat of his soldiers, they gradually closed in upon and completely surrounded him.   Twice before this, he had been wounded ; but, in the excitement of the battle, and the vast importance of his own presence among his men, he had paid no attention to them.   Now, however, surrounded and completely overpowered by a crowd of the enemy, he endeavoured to force his way by the bayonet ; but, while doing so, a shot passed through his heart, and the tall figure that had so often led the van in battle was seen to fall from his horse ; and, when his men gently raised him again into his saddle, he fell down among their hands and expired.   Keith's last battle was over ; his fightings were suddenly ended ; the death the soldier loves to die had come to him at last.   Over his dead body, both Austrians and Prussians fought until the latter were driven back and compelled to retire to the heights of Dresa. There, on the Saturday, they were attacked by the Duke of Aremberg, and, after a fierce conflict of five hours' duration, were forced again to retire.   Then it was that Frederick saw the full force of Keith's remonstrances ; for, besides having 9000 men killed or wounded, he had lost his best general, and he himself and almost all his generals were wounded.

" Croats," says Carlyle, " had the plundering of Keith ;

other Austrians, not of Croat kind, carried the general into
Hochkirch church.   On the morrow—Sunday, Oct. 15,
—Keith had honourable soldier's burial there, 'twelve
cannon' salvoing thrice, and 'the whole corps of Colloredo'
with their muskets thrice,—Lacy as chief mourner, not
without tears.   Four months after, by royal order, Keith's
body was conveyed to Berlin ; reinterred in Berlin, in a
still more solemn, public manner, with all the honours,
all the regrets ; and Keith sleeps now in Garniston-Kirche,
far from bonnie Inverugie—the hoarse sea-winds and
caverns of Dunottar singing vague requiem to his honourable line and him."

   " Thus disappeared one of the greatest men of the
age ;—a man worthy to be compared with those illustrious
names which raised Greece and ancient Rome to all their
height of glory.   His countenance was expressive of his
character ; his stature rather above the middle size, but of
a make extremely well proportioned ; his complexion
brown, eyebrows thick, and his features very agreeable ;
but, above all, he had an air of so much goodness that it
quite gained the heart at his very first appearance.   His
demeanour was like that of a respectable father of a family,
which challenged reverence, but much more strongly
challenged love ; his constitution was remarkably vigorous
till weakened by the incredible fatigues which he under-
went, yet the vigour of his spirit far surpassed that of his
body.   He would have made a great figure in the sciences
and in literature, had not his life been so much occupied in
the manner we have seen.   Nevertheless, there have been

few generals so eminent as he was in this respect. He
spoke English, French, Spanish, Russian, Swedish, and
Latin, and was able to read the Greek authors. His
ordinary conversation was in French, in which language
he expressed himself perfectly well, and with great preci-
sion, being one that did not speak much. He had seen
all the courts of Europe, great and small, from that at
Avignon to the residence of the Khan of Tartary, and
accommodated himself to every place as if it had been his
native country. General, minister, courtier, philosopher,—
all these characters, however different in themselves, were
in him united. The most profound scholars have been
known to leave his company quite in an ecstacy, and
scarcely believing their own ears." Such are the remarks
of M. Formey, a Royal Acadamician, in a discourse on the
death of Marshal Keith, delivered by him in the year 1760.
So eager were the inhabitants of Berlin to see this just
and admiring estimate of their illustrious governor, that
they would not wait for its regular appearance in the
records of the Academy, but demanded its immediate
publication. It makes the hearts of Britons—and particularly Scotchmen—swell with noble pride when they
listen to such remarks from foreigners, and behold their
gratitude "for the benefits which they derived from his
virtues, and the admiration with which they reviewed his
numerous and brave exploits."

CONCLUSION.

And so passed away the last of the Keiths. After shedding a lustre and glory over their country for more than 500 years, and being engaged in the most important services, civil and military, they faded away from the annals of our country in a cause the most despicable, and for a king the most worthless that could well be imagined—one to whom, in every respect, they were infinitely superior. And yet what might have been supposed to have been their ruin was, in reality, the means of rendering them still more widely famous, and handing down their names to posterity connected with the most famous men and most noble exploits of the greatest countries of Europe. After wandering as strangers and foreigners over the greater part of the Continent seeking rest for their weary feet, they at last found the work assigned to them ; and, by their conscientious discharge of it, their straightforward conduct, and their undaunted courage, earned a good report and a noble reward among men. After remaining for a time in comparative obscurity, they at last set in a full blaze of glory,—the one the representative of the military glory of his race ; the other, of the wisdom, temperance, and equability of temper for which it was also remarkable. The vigour of a series of generations seems to have been concentrated in the persons of the men who formed the final link. They mingled, in their exile, with men and

kings much more illustrious than the Hanoverian race that
then filled the British throne. With these they lived on terms
of the closest intimacy, and counted them as their familiar
friends. No one was more respected than the Field-
Marshal, no one more loved and esteemed than the old Earl.

Both were concise and elegant writers, a fact attributable,
in some measure, to their early training under their relation
Bishop Keith. In the purity and elegance of their diction,
they form a great contrast to the majority of their contemporaries, particularly the young pretender, Charles Edward
Stuart, as may readily be seen from an examination of the
Stuart paper. The Field-Marshal wrote a series of letters
to Lords G. and E. Drummond, concerning the Russian
Empire—1748, 1755, 1756—which were sold, in 1844,
at the sale of the library of the Duke of Sussex. He has
also left us a fragment of an autobiography " which, for
raciness of style, chasteness of language, and graphic
power of writing, can scarcely be excelled in literature,"
and which makes us only regret that he did not finish it.
We long, in vain, for some insight—such as he could have
given us—into that private life of the great Frederick, with
which he was so well acquainted ; and for a description,
from his graphic pen, of that tour which they made
together in disguise through a great part of Germany,
Poland, and Hungary. "Sagacious, skilful, imperturbable,
without fear, and without noise, a man quietly ever ready,"
Frederick "appreciated his talents, enjoyed his social
qualities, and what with him was rarer, never laid aside
for a moment the respect due to his character."

In an age, and among a people remarkable for their disregard of religion, the two were firm and resolute in adhering to the Protestant faith, and for no wordly advantage would they renounce the tenets of their youth. In soldiers of fortune, this, to say the least of it, was very remarkable, and proves that, even in exile, they remembered that the motto borne by their ancestors and themselves was *Veritas Vincit*, Truth Conquers. In the strict Roman Catholic court of the Pretender, they must have often felt themselves peculiarly situated; and yet, by neither, do we ever find them referring to their strange position unless incidentally, when necessity compels them, or when their adherence to it became a barrier to their advancement.

It is not to be expected that the Prussian nation would dwell largely on the deeds of a stranger, or grant to him the glory of their mighty deeds; and yet, either from the prominence of his position, the eminence of his actions, or the real love entertained for him, he holds a much higher place in the affections of the people, and appears oftener in the histories and biographies of the time, than most foreigners. He was the favourite of a king who had no respect of persons, and who valued a man for his worth alone. His promptness of action, his watchfulness, his conscientious discharge of every duty devolving upon him however menial, his care of his soldiers, his personal courage—on many occasions he himself leading on his men to victory,—his fertility of resources, and his unobtrusive behaviour on all occasions won him the hearts of all!. He bore, with excellent patience, the shameful treatment he received in Spain; the intriguing, the ill-usuage, the obnoxious and insulting preference of Russia; and, latterly, the harsh words and hasty remarks of Frederick, who, however, made up for his momentary ill-temper by future expressions of confidence and affection. He had few personal enemies, and these arose more from his success than from any fault of his own. He seems to have made friends wherever he went; for, during the whole of the long life which he spent in foreign countries, we only find one—Prince Maurice of Dessau—who was really his enemy, and endeavoured to slander him to Frederick. But Keith, free from all jealousy, and straightforward in all his actions, treated this reckless young man with the silent contempt he merited.

But what seems to have endeared him most both to his own soldiers and to those over whom he at various times held sway, was the mildness of his rule, and his horror and detestation of all unnecessary cruelty. Many instances may be given of this during his career in Russia, where the wars were prosecuted in the barbarous manner characteristic of a former age. "He never omitted to do anything in his power that might soften and alleviate the calamities of war, lessen the number of its miseries, and, in some measure, relieve those whom it had rendered wretched." Algarotti, Frederick's Lord Chamberlain, who must have had many opportunities of judging of Keith, says, regarding this same subject:—"Keith, a man of excellent judgment, who, by the sweetness and mildness of his manners, procured more submission to his orders from the Russian officers than any other could obtain by severity. In the midst of arms he did not neglect letters, and to the practice of war, joined the most profound theory."

His manners were courteous and elegant, and his behaviour on state occasions such as to prove that the most intrepid warrior may also be the most polished courtier. As instances of this, we may mention his conduct at the court of Poland, and the golden opinions which he gained for himself from all classes in Sweden, when he went on the very disagreeable duty of overawing the people.

But, most of all, he excelled in military affairs. One has only to take a glimpse at his history, or to read carefully the Russian and Seven Years' Wars, to see what a prominent part he took in them, and to find his impress on Europe. As instances of his military genius, we might, with confidence, point to the siege of Ockzakow, where he is said to have been the first to mount the breach ; the battles of Williamstrand, Rossbach, and Hochkirchen ; and the celebrated retreats from Prague and Olmutz before forces infinitely superior to his own.

At the head of the Prussian forces he, no doubt, had many opportunities of enriching himself, yet we find him dying poor. His brother, writing to Madame Geoffrin, on the death of the Field-Marshal, says :—" My brother has left me a splendid heritage. He came to impose a tax on the whole of Bohemia at the head of a grand army, and I have only found seventy ducats in his purse." Well might the same person write, when requested by M. Formey to supply him with materials for a biography,

"*Probus vixit, fortis obiit,*" He lived a pure life, and died a brave death.

It is not to be wondered at that Prussia honoured such a man by erecting a monument to his memory. In the Wilhelm Platz, close to the Potsdam gate, on a pedestal of polished Swedish red granite, stands the statue of Keith, erected by his master and friend Frederick the Great, in the uniform of a Prussian marshal, with a scroll in his hand. The original in marble was removed because it was getting spoiled by exposure to the air, and a bronze one, of which the Peterhead statue is an exact copy, was erected in its place. And in the church of Hochkirchen, near which he fell and was at first buried, his cousin Sir Robert Murray Keith placed a monument—a modest urn of black marble on a pedestal of grey. Concerning it he says :—"Lord Marischal has agreed to my erecting a decent gravestone to the memory of his late brother, and in the place where he fell. They sent me two inscriptions, but they were long and languid. I have engaged Baron Hagen and his friend Metastasio to touch me up something manly and energetic ; and, in the course of the summer, my tribute of veneration for the memory of a brave and honest man will be recorded in monumental marble." The inscription is to the following effect :—

"To James Keith (son of William, hereditary Earl Marischal of the kingdom of Scotland, and Mary Drummond), the highest general of the army of Frederick, the king of the Prussians,—a man famous for his ancient morals and military valour, who, while he was endeavouring to restore his line that had been forced in a battle fought not far from this place, fell, fighting as a hero ought, on the 14th October, 1758."

It is the memory of such a man as we have attempted to portray that the King of Prussia, after the lapse of rather more than a century, has delighted to honour. Originally at the request of a private individual, he has presented to the town of Peterhead the exact duplicate of the Statue which stands in Wilhelm Platz, and which is now erected in the principal street of the town founded by his ancestors, and near to which he himself was born. Proud of the honour conferred upon them, and still prouder of having given birth to a man whose memory and good deeds remain green and flagrant even until now, they will look upon this present as a link that will more closely unite the country of his birth with that of his adoption, and regard it as an augury of the future brotherhood of nations. And when they gaze upon it, and think of the great talents, the splendid courage, the perfect integrity, the disinterested conduct, and the patient endurance which marked his character, may they profit by his example, and in the work which God has assigned them—go and do likewise.

THE END.

NOTES.

p. 11.   *Induced by their mother.*

As an instance of the strong Jacobite feeling of the mother of the last of the Marischals, we may give a story related by Norval Clyne, Esq., in his lecture on the " Poetry of the Jacobites ":—" I have heard a story, worth telling here, of Lady Keith, thus left lonely in her ' castle by the sea.' She had a maid-servant, who, previously to 1715, had married and gone to live elsewhere; but who returned to visit her old mistress after the calamitous result of the rising. On her venturing to express to the Countess her regret that the young lords had taken a course so ruinous to their family, the noble dame instantly rose from her seat, with kindling looks, and said—' Woman ! if my sons had not done what they did, I would have gone out myself with my spindle and my rock." '

p. 12.   *It is right to state that this rests on every insufficient evidence, &c.*

Since writing the life of Marshal Keith, I have met with a curious anecdote strongly confirmatory of the opinion there given of the Earl Marischal's conduct on this important occasion. I had drawn my conclusions from his after course in life, and from certain hints to be found in the Stuart Papers. The Earl did not *offer* to proclaim King James at the head of his troops ; but *influence* was brought to bear upon him to induce him to do so. The fact is, every one of the Jacobite leaders was anxious that the thing should be done ; *but each wished some other one than himself to do it.*

" When Queen Anne was dying, Mr Scott of Brotherstown, a colonel of the Guards, was on guard at the palace that night on which the queen died. He went to Dr Arbuthnot, one of the queen's physicians, and desired the doctor ' to tell him whenever the queen was dead,' but the doctor told him ' that he durst not.' Upon this, the colonel desired the doctor ' to let him know by the sign of putting to the window a white handkerchief,' to which the doctor agreed. As soon as the queen was dead, Dr Arbuthnot gave the sign, upon which the colonel went to the Earl Marischal's house and desired to see him immediately. The servant told the colonel ' that he was forbid to admit any person to his lordship till his bell was rung, as he was late up the night before, and it was yet very early in the morning ;' but the colonel insisted upon being admitted, as he had matters of great consequence to communicate to his lordship. He locked the room door and then awaked his lordship, and desired him ' to rise immediately and proclaim the king, as the queen, his sister, was dead, which none out of the palace knew but him.' His lordship said ' there might be danger in doing it ;' but the colonel said ' there would be none, if they did it without loss of time.' He assured his lordship, ' if he would draw out the guards immediately, and proclaim the king (James Stuart) at Charing-Cross, he knew the Duke of Ormond was ready to do the same at the head of the army, and that he would take upon himself to secure the Tower ;' but his lordship remained quite obstinate and said ' that it might cost them their lives if they failed in the attempt.' But the colonel repeated his assurance ' that there was not the least fear, if done immediately,' and ' although they lost their lives, it was losing them in an honourable way ;' and ' gave his word of honour that, if they were brought to a trial, he would do all in his power to save his lordship's life, and would declare, when on the scaffold, that it was by his persuasion his lordship did it, he being a young man.' But all was to no purpose ; he remained quite obstinate, and would do nothing ; at which the colonel left him in a great passion. This conference was not known until after the battle of Sheriffmuir. Dr Arbuthnot asked at Colonel Scott some time after, 'What he meant by being so particular about the queen's death?' but the colonel would not tell the doctor. When Earl Marischal was retreating after the battle of Sheriffmuir, in company with Mr Irvine of Brackly, they being very much fatigued, his lordship threw himself down on the ground, and burst out a crying, which surprised Mr Irvine greatly, who bade his lordship 'not lose courage, as he hoped soon to get to some place where they would get rest and refreshment.' His lordship replied 'that it was not the fatigue they had undergone that day that distressed him, but that he had to answer for the death of all the men that were killed that day. Had he taken Colonel Scott's advice at Queen Anne's death, he might have saved his country by restoring the king when it was in his power.' And, although 'we had then failed I *would* have died with honour; whereas, I *will* die now like a dog, unregretted;' upon which he told Mr Irvine the whole conference that passed between Colonel Scott and him at the queen's death, which surprised Mr Irvine extremely. Mr Irvine told this to Mr Ogilvie of Balbignie, Colonel Scott's half-brother; and to Mr Peter Smith, Methuen's brother. Some time after, Colonel Scott came to Balbignie, where he met Mr Irvine and Mr Peter Smith. Mr Ogilvie, in presence of these gentlemen, asked the colonel 'if the above conference had passed between the Earl Marischal and him at Queen Anne's death?' The colonel confessed it had; 'but desired it might not be spoke of while he lived, as it might lose him his commission, he being still in the army.'"—*Strickland's Lives of the Queens of England. Vol. VIII., p.p. 533-534.*

p. 77. *Originally at the request of a private individual, &c.*

Here we shall endeavour to give a short account of how this statue was obtained for Peterhead. The circumstances connected with it are so interesting and peculiar that they deserve more than a passing notice. In 1865, Mr Anderson, the late editor of the *Sentinel*, paid a visit to Prussia, and while in Berlin learned that the original statue of Keith, in marble, by Tassaert, had been removed and was lying in the Museum of Sculpture. On his return he threw out the hint—"What would the Peterhead folk say to ask the marble from the Prussian government? This request might be an unusual one; but there is no saying that it might not be granted." Acting upon this suggestion, Mr Ingram, who at the time was a member of the Town Council, brought the subject before that body. In October 1866, he suggested that the Town Council and the Burgh Member should exert themselves to obtain the statue for the town. At the time they were unanimous regarding it; but, upon enquiry, it was found that the said statue had been duly placed in the Prussian Military Academy; and, thereupon, the subject was dropped by the civic dignitaries at least. Mr Ingram, after waiting a considerable period, did what he had originally intended,—wrote to Count Bismarck himself; and, though it was a very unusual course, and one unlikely to succeed, yet the result exceeded even his most sanguine expectations. He has, indeed, very much reason to be proud of his share in this matter. Unfortunately we cannot give a copy of Mr Ingram's letter to Count Bismarck, as the original draft of it was destroyed. This deficiency has, to a certain extent, been remedied by the following account given by him of its contents. He said—"My argument all along was, that by making such a request, we were doing no mean thing. I believed, as the result has proved, that the king of Prussia would consider it an honour to have the opportunity of gratifying the request. At the time of the Bruce, when Scotland was ruled over by Edward of England, and on the glorious event of our victories, had we then received the help of a native of Prussia, as Marshal Keith had helped Frederick the Great, we would not have done less than was done by the people of Prussia in honour of our countryman; and would we not have considered it a privilege of a high kind, as a nation, to have had an opportunity of gratifying such a request as was made by us, which, I am happy to say, has been so gracefully responded to. Now that the liberties of our country are secured, we look back with pride on the noble deeds of our ancestors." After waiting nearly three months, a reply came from the Prussian Ambassador at London to the following effect:—

"Prussian Embassy, London, May 9, 1868.

"Sir.—I am desired by Count Bismarck to inform you that His Excellency received your letter of the 17th February last, in which you privately expressed the wish that the statue in marble of the famous Field-Marshal Keith, which had sometime ago been taken down at Berlin and replaced by one of bronze, might be given over to Peterhead, his native town,—as a statue of Keith, if given you by the Prussian nation would be of tenfold value to one which the city of Peterhead itself could set up of him.

"Your request was sure to meet with a sympathetic reception on the part of His Majesty's Government, as the highly gifted Scotch historian who with such a thorough appreciation wrote the history of our great king, and thereby erected to his Generals (and amongst these to Field-Marshal Keith) a worthy historical monument, has long since understood, as your request proves, to form between his native land and Prussia a spiritual tie to which His Majesty's Government would willingly give a lasting expression by the erection of a statue of Keith in the Scotch seaport.

"It was, therefore, to Count Bismarck an agreeable duty to suggest to His Majesty to comply with your request; and, I am happy to say, his intercession has met with the most gracious reception on the part of the King.

"The original statue of Keith, however, which, together with the other statues in marble of the heroes of the Seven Years' War, has been set up within the walls of the Military School at Berlin, cannot be withdrawn from this destination. But His Majesty has ordered the casting of a statue of the Field-Marshal for Peterhead, after the still existing model in plaster which was made for the purpose of casting the statue in bronze now standing on the Wilhelms-Platz at Berlin.

"Having thus stated to you the preliminary result of your private letter to Count Bismarck, I venture to suggest that the best way in which this affair might be brought to a satisfactory conclusion would be that the Corporation of Peterhead, confidentially informed by you of the King's favourable disposition, should direct an official address to him, in which they beg his Majesty to be graciously pleased to favour their town with a statue of the celebrated Field-Marshal Keith, in honour of the place that gave him birth.—I am, Sir, your obedient servant,

"Count BERNSTORFF,
"His Prussian Majesty's Ambassador."

"Alexander Ingram, Esq., Peterhead."

To this Mr Ingram replied—

"Peterhead, 15th May, 1868.
"The Honourable Count Bernstorff.

"May it please your Excellency, I had the honour to receive Your Excellency's letter of the 9th curt., containing the most gratifying intelligence that His Majesty the King of Prussia would be graciously pleased, on the application of the Magistrates and Council, to present this Burgh with a casting of the statue of our eminent townsman, the famous Marshal Keith.

"I have met in council with the Magistrates, and, as you have intimated, have confidentially communicated to them your wish that His Prussian Majesty should be approached by memorial, or petition, praying that Peterhead may be presented by His Majesty with a Statue of the grand old Marshal. And I have much pleasure in saying that a petition is immediately to be prepared and sent to you, when, without doubt, you will take the proper steps to forward it to your Government.

"I now beg most respectfully to thank Your Excellency for your suggestions and explanations in your letter. I know the community of Peterhead will feel proud of the gracious consideration, patriotism, and gratitude the illustrious King of Prussia will show, by presenting a Statue of Marshal Keith, which will be placed on a pedestal of our famous local granite, in front of the Town-Hall, and on the pedestal will be inscribed, in suitable terms, that the Statue was given to us by your noble King and enlightened nation, in gratitude, and as a recognition of the estimation in which the Prussians at the present time hold the heroic deeds of Frederick the Great, and his Scotch Marshal Keith.—I have the honour to be, Your Excellency's most humble servant,

"ALEXANDER INGRAM."

Acting upon the Count's suggestion, a meeting of the Town Council was held, and the following memorial, drawn up by the Town-Clerk, was forwarded to the King of Prussia:—

"To His Most Gracious Majesty the King of Prussia.

"The humble petition of the Provost, Magistrates, and Town Council of the Burgh of Peterhead, in the County of Aberdeen, in North Britain,

"Sheweth,—That it has come to your Petitioners' knowledge that the original statue, erected in Wilhelms-Platz, Berlin, in commemoration of the illustrious Field-Marshal Keith, has been removed, and that a new one of bronze has been substituted. Your Petitioners, therefore, with all humility, venture to approach Your Majesty with an expression of their high gratification of this renewed mark of appreciation of long departed worth, more especially as the object was not a native of Prussia.

"But this approach to Your Majesty is not altogether unselfish, inasmuch as your Petitioners presume most respectfully to bring under Your Majesty's notice the facts that Peterhead was founded by a member of the ancient and noble family of Keith, and that the warlike Marshal and his eminent brother, the Earl Marischal, the Superior of the town, were both born in its immediate vicinity. From these considerations, it has seemed to your Petitioners that Your Majesty might not be indisposed to honour this community by presenting them with a Statue of Marshal Keith, similar to that erected in Wilhelms-Platz, Berlin, to be placed in the principal street of this, his ancestral town, to commemorate the glory and martial achievements of one whose memory is deservedly held in esteem by all civilized nations.

"Should it, therefore, please Your Majesty graciously to comply with this somewhat unusual request, it would be held as a great boon by your Petitioners and their constituents, and not only by them, but they believe that the gift would be highly prized throughout the land, as evidencing the desire of Your Majesty that good feeling and amity should subsist between two nations so highly civilized, and whose commercial interests are so closely interwoven.

"Whereby your Petitioners humbly pray that Your Majesty will favourably consider what is above set forth, and be graciously pleased to cause a Statue of Field-Marshal James Francis Edward Keith, to be presented to the Petitioners for behoof of the community over which they preside, to be erected in the principal street in this Burgh, as a memorial of a townsman of whom they are proud, and as a recognition of the services of a chivalrous Scotchman by a mighty people, whose battles he fought under Your Majesty's ancestor—the renowned King of Prussia—Frederick the Great.

"And your Petitioners will ever pray.

"Signed in name and by appointment of the Magistrates and Town Council of Peterhead, in Council assembled, and the common seal of the Burgh affixed hereunto this 14th day of May, 1868.

"WILLM. ALEXANDER,
"Provost and Chief Magistrate of Peterhead."

To this there came the following reply:—

"Prussian Embassy, London, September 7, 1868.

"SIR,—According to instructions received from the Government of the King, I have the honour to inform you that His Prussian Majesty, on the petition presented to him by the Magistrates and Town Council of Peterhead, on the 14th of May last, has been graciously pleased to bestow upon that city, by an Order of Cabinet, dated the 23d of August, 1868, the requested statue of Field-Marshal, J. F. E. Keith.

"Enclosing herewith a certified copy of this order, I am happy to further inform you that the statue is already approaching its completion, and that it will be addressed to you, as, besides your capacity of Town-Clerk, you have also that of Vice-Consul of Prussia at Peterhead. Of the sending of the statue in question from Berlin to Peterhead, you will be advised by me in due time.—I have the honour to be, sir, your obedient servant,

"KATTE, Prussian Chargé d'Affaires."
"Al. Robertson, Esq., Town-Clerk's Office, Peterhead."

(Translation of Order from His Majesty.)

"Coblentz, 23d August, 1868.

"I received, with particular satisfaction, the representation of the Provost, Magistrates, and Town Council of the worthy town of Peterhead, that the memory of Field-Marshal J. F. E. Keith and his heroic career in Prussia still live in his native place. I, therefore, willingly bestow on the town of Peterhead the wished-for statue of the Field-Marshal, after the model of the monument which my great ancestor ordered to be placed to his deserving General in Berlin; and hope that this statue may contribute to maintain lasting relationship between the birth land of the Field-Marshal and his adopted home, Prussia.

"With the execution of the present gift-order I charge you, the Minister of Foreign Affairs.

"(Signed)   WILHELM.
"For the Minister of Foreign Affairs.

"(Signed)   GR. EULENBURG."

About the end of the same month, a letter came from the Prussian Chargé d'Affaires, London, informing the Town Council that the statue was on its way:—

"Prussian Embassy, London, September 24, 1868.

"Al. Robertson, Esq., Town-Clerk's Office, Peterhead.

"SIR,—With reference to my letter of the 7th instant, I beg to inform you that the Statue of Field-Marshal J. F. E. Keith, which His Majesty the King of Prussia has been graciously pleased to bestow upon the City of Peterhead, will be sent from Hamburg to Leith by steamer on the 30th of this month, by the Berlin firm Thaland and Dietrich. From Leith to Peterhead it will also be forwarded by steamer. The Statue will be packed in a case, marked in German 'Statue des Feldmarschalls Keith für die Stadt Peterhead, Schottland;' and this case will be addressed to you. The sending will be free from charges.

"I addressed to-day the necessary application to Lord Stanley, Her Majesty's principal Secretary of State for Foreign Affairs, for the duty-free, and, if possible, unopened entry of the case in question.

"Requesting you to inform me in due time of the arrival of the Statue at Peterhead, I have the honour to be, sir, your obedt. servt.,

"KATTE, Prussian Chargé d'Affaires."

It arrived safely at its destination on the 6th October, 1868, and now adorns our Tolbooth Green—an honour and an ornament to our bustling little town. When looking on it, the inhabitants cannot but remember the great kindness of a King who granted such a work of art on the representation of a private individual, and feel grateful to a country which has for more than a century retained the memory of the noble deeds of one who was born in their neighbourhood.

The pedestal bears the following inscription :—" Field-Marshal Keith, born at Inverugie, 1696; killed at the battle of Hochkirchen, 14th October, 1758. The gift of William I., King of Prussia, to the town of Peterhead, August 1868. *Probus vixit, fortis obiit.*"

PETERHEAD:
PRINTED AT THE "SENTINEL" OFFICE,
BROAD PLACE.